PUFFIN BOOKS

Editor: Kaye Webb

A BOOK OF PRINCESSES

There is a time to read stories about people like yourself, and a time to read about people who are different. That is when you should read about princesses, for whether they are bullied or cherished, proud or simple, hardworking or spoilt, beautiful or long-nosed, they are always special.

In this book you will find every type of princess imaginable; some are nice, some are horrid, some pretty, some plain, and the stories about them have been told by such wonderful writers as Walter de la Mare, Hans Andersen, Oscar Wilde, Charles Dickens, A. A. Milne, and George MacDonald.

It is a book for little girls, especially those who like to dream.

A BOOK OF
PRINCESSES

SELECTED BY
SALLY PATRICK JOHNSON

ILLUSTRATED BY
FRITZ WEGNER

PUFFIN BOOKS

Puffin Books, Penguin Books Ltd,
Harmondsworth, Middlesex, England
Penguin Books Australia Ltd, Ringwood, Victoria, Australia

—

First published by Hamish Hamilton 1963
Published in Puffin Books 1965
Reprinted 1967, 1971 (twice), 1975

—

Copyright © Sally Patrick Johnson, 1962, 1963
Illustrations copyright © Fritz Wegner, 1963

—

Made and printed in Great Britain by
Cox & Wyman Ltd,
London, Reading and Fakenham
Set in Monotype Fournier

CONTENTS

INTRODUCTION

THERE are not as many real Princesses in the world as there once were, but those who remain still make headlines and inspire love and curiosity in ordinary people. Even the most commonplace events – when they happen to a Princess – take on glamour and excitement. To young and old alike, the Princess symbolizes something special, and stories of Princesses in this modern age have the same appeal they must have had in the vanished days of peasants and nobles.

Perhaps this is because, of all the members of the Royal Family, the Princess represents our dreams of beauty, wealth, and privilege most perfectly. In fiction, at least, she is without pressing responsibility, free to be pampered, adored, enchanted, kidnapped, rescued, and won in all enviable combinations. She is the classic figure to mount upon a pedestal. There is a mystical something about her that inspires awe, love, and even fanatic devotion, be it in the public, the Prince, or the writer. And when she is wicked, her treachery is all the more horrible and her downfall all the more deserved.

The Queen, by contrast, rarely attains this stature. In most stories she is either a wicked stepmother, a quaintly doting parent, or an efficient housekeeper: an instrument. The King is often rash, usually distracted and busy, and for ever worrying about an heir for his throne. The Prince is invariably off slaying dragons, and very likely on his way to rescue a Princess. And so the Princess herself is left to be the centre of countless intrigues, recipient of fantastic gifts, object of widely assorted suitors, more lovely than any other Princess before or since, and eternally the ideal of romantic femininity.

This sense of the special wonder of the Princess is found in the earliest literature and was probably alive even before books were written. Such Princess stories as those collected by Hans Andersen, Madame d'Aulnoy, and the brothers Grimm in the nineteenth century are mainly folk tales which go back almost to the dawn of history. In the late 1800s a number of professional writers began to turn their hands to the creation of new stories. Though these works sometimes contained elements of folk tales, the old devices were usually given a fresh, often satirical twist. Most important, the writing was marked by greater originality and sense of style, deeper feeling for character, and more professional ability to plot than had been seen before. So the tradition of the Princess story of folklore was enriched by a tradition of the literary Princess story. Not only have writers for children such as A. A. Milne, E. Nesbit, and George MacDonald contributed to this later tradition, but also writers better known for their adult works – Charles Dickens, Oscar Wilde, W. Somerset Maugham, James Thurber, and many others.

The stories in this book are chosen from among the best of both the folk and the literary Princess stories. There are, however, some stories (or, perhaps more accurately, plots or themes of stories) which are so familiar as to be part of almost everyone's experience, and these have been omitted. 'Sleeping Beauty', 'The White Cat', 'The Frog Prince', 'Snow White', and 'Beauty and the Beast' have appeared in too many collections of fairy tales to need inclusion here. On the other hand, a brilliant or unusual adaptation of an old favourite – such as Walter de la Mare's 'The Dancing Princesses', or Ruth Sawyer's 'The Princess and the Vagabone' – could not be passed over. The single exception to the rule of avoiding the too familiar is the very brief original version of 'The Princess on the Pea', which, for every reason, seemed the ideal story with which to begin the book.

Despite the fact that each story is about a Princess or Princesses, the selections encompass a wide variety of styles, moods, and plots, to say nothing of types of Princesses – most good, some outrageous, and one absolutely wicked. It was the editor's intent to prepare a feast rather than a surfeit, and to bring to parent and child the pleasures of some of the world's best story-telling.

S.P.J.

THE PRINCESS ON THE PEA

HANS CHRISTIAN ANDERSEN

We begin with a story by Hans Christian Andersen, the world's most famous teller of fairy tales. His short account of 'The Princess on the Pea' is the best-known of all Princess stories. It has often been retold, sometimes entitled 'The Real Princess', with many more frills and details, and has even been made into a musical comedy, *Once Upon a Mattress*, but in this book we are using the original version. It will show you one of the many characteristics of a Princess, and when you have read some of the stories about Princesses who are less delicate, you will see how much these Royal people have changed in the course of literary history.

T HERE was once a Prince who wanted to marry a Princess; but she was to be a *real* Princess. So he travelled about, all through the world, to find a real one, but everywhere there was something in the way. There were Princesses enough, but whether they were *real* Princesses he could not quite make out: there was always something that did not seem quite right. So he came home again, and was quite sad, for he wished so much to have a real Princess.

One evening a terrible storm came on. It lightninged and thundered, the rain streamed down; it was quite fearful! Then there was a knocking at the town gate, and the old King went out to open it.

It was a Princess who stood outside the gate. But, mercy! How she looked, from the rain and the rough weather! The water ran down from her hair and her clothes; it ran in at the points of her shoes and out at the heels; and yet she declared that she was a real Princess.

'Yes, we will soon find that out,' thought the old Queen. But she said nothing, only went into the bedchamber, took all the bedding off and put a pea on the flooring of the bedstead; then she took twenty mattresses and laid them upon the pea, and then twenty eiderdown beds upon the mattresses. On this the Princess had to lie all night. In the morning she was asked how she had slept.

'Oh, miserably!' said the Princess. 'I scarcely closed my eyes all night long. Goodness knows what was in my bed. I lay upon something hard, so that I am black and blue all over. It is quite dreadful!'

Now they saw that she was a real Princess, for through the twenty mattresses and the twenty eiderdown beds she had felt the pea. No one but a real Princess could be so delicate.

So the Prince took her for his wife, for now he knew that he had a true Princess; and the pea was put in the museum, and it is there now, unless somebody has carried it off.

Look you, this is a true story.

A TOY PRINCESS

MARY DE MORGAN

Mary de Morgan was one of the first writers to invent new plots for fairy tales instead of simply retelling the old ones. Writing in the time of Queen Victoria, when everyone was supposed to be very polite, she saw that extreme politeness was not always the best thing, and this gave her an idea for a story about a Princess and a clever machine. We see that 'the public' may have one idea of what is proper, but that Miss de Morgan has quite another.

MORE than a thousand years ago, in a country quite on the other side of the world, it fell out that the people all grew so very polite that they hardly ever spoke to each other. And they never said more than was quite necessary, as 'Just so', 'Yes, indeed', 'Thank you', and 'If you please.' And it was thought to be the rudest thing in the world for anyone to say they liked or disliked, or loved or hated, or were happy or miserable. No one ever laughed aloud, and if anyone had been seen to cry they would at once have been avoided by their friends.

The King of this country married a Princess from a neighbouring land who was very good and beautiful, but the people in her own home were as unlike her husband's people as it was possible to be. They laughed and talked, and were noisy and merry when they were happy, and cried and lamented if they were sad. In fact, whatever they felt they showed at once, and the Princess was just like them.

So when she came to her new home, she could not at all understand her subjects, or make out why there was no shouting and cheering to welcome her and why everyone was so distant and formal. After a time, when she found they never changed but were always the same, just as stiff and quiet, she wept and began to pine for her own old home.

Every day she grew thinner and paler. The courtiers were much too polite to notice how ill their young Queen looked, but she knew it herself and believed she was going to die.

Now, she had a fairy godmother, named Taboret, whom she loved very dearly and who was always kind to her. When she knew her end was drawing near, she sent for her godmother and had a long talk with her quite alone.

No one knew what was said, and soon afterwards a little Princess was born and the Queen died. Of course all the courtiers were sorry for the poor Queen's death, but it would have been thought rude to say so. So, although there was a grand funeral and the court put on mourning, everything else went on much as it had done before.

The little baby was christened Ursula and given to some court ladies to be taken charge of. Poor little Princess! *She* cried hard enough, and nothing could stop her.

All her ladies were frightened and said that they had not heard such a dreadful noise for a long time. But till she was about two years old, nothing could stop her crying when she was cold or hungry, or crowing when she was pleased.

After that she began to understand a little what was meant when her nurses told her, in cold, polite tones, that she was being naughty, and she grew much quieter.

She was a pretty little girl with a round baby face and big merry blue eyes; but as she grew older, her eyes grew less and less merry and bright, and her fat little face grew thin and pale. She was not allowed to play with any other children, lest she might learn bad manners; and she was not taught any games or given any toys. So she passed most of her time, when she was not at her lessons, looking out of the window at the birds flying against the clear blue sky; and sometimes she would give a sad little sigh when her ladies were not listening.

One day the old fairy Taboret made herself invisible and flew over to the King's palace to see how things were going on there. She went straight up to the nursery, where she found poor little Ursula sitting by the window with her head leaning on her hand.

It was a very grand room, but there were no toys or dolls about, and when the fairy saw this, she frowned to herself and shook her head.

'Your Royal Highness's dinner is now ready,' said the head nurse to Ursula.

'I don't want any dinner,' said Ursula without turning her head.

'I think I have told Your Royal Highness before that it is not polite to say you don't want anything or that you don't like it,' said the nurse. 'We are waiting for Your Royal Highness.'

So the Princess got up and went to the dinner table, and Taboret watched them all the time. When she saw how pale little Ursula was, and how little she ate, and that there was no talking or laughing allowed, she sighed and frowned even more than before, and then she flew back to her fairy home, where she sat for some hours in deep thought.

At last she rose and went out to pay a visit to the largest shop in Fairyland.

It was a queer sort of shop. It was neither a grocer's nor a draper's nor a hatter's. Yet it contained sugar and dresses and hats. But the sugar was magic sugar which transformed any liquid into which it was put; the dresses each had some special charm; and the hats were wishing caps. It was, in fact, a shop where every sort of spell or charm was sold.

Into this shop Taboret flew; and as she was well known there as a good customer, the master of the shop came forward to meet her at once and, bowing, begged to know what he could get for her.

'I want', said Taboret, 'a Princess.'

'A Princess!' said the shopman, who was in reality an old wizard. 'What size do you want it? I have one or two in stock.'

'It must look now about six years old. But it must grow.'

'I can make you one,' said the wizard, 'but it'll come rather expensive.'

'I don't mind that,' said Taboret. 'See! I want it to look exactly like this,' and, so saying, she took a portrait of Ursula out of her bosom and gave it to the old man, who examined it carefully.

'I'll get it for you,' he said. 'When will you want it?'

'As soon as possible,' said Taboret. 'By tomorrow evening if possible. How much will it cost?'

'It'll come to a good deal,' said the wizard thoughtfully. 'I have such difficulty in getting these things properly made in these days. What sort of a voice is it to have?'

'It need not be at all talkative,' said Taboret, 'so that won't add much to the price. It need only say, "If you please", "No thank you", "Certainly", and "Just so".'

'Well, under those circumstances,' said the wizard, 'I will do it for four cat's footfalls, two fish's screams and two swan's songs.'

'It is too much,' cried Taboret. 'I'll give you the footfalls and the screams, but to ask for swan's songs!'

She did not really think it dear, but she always made a point of trying to beat tradesmen down.

'I can't do it for less,' said the wizard, 'and if you think it too much, you'd better try another shop.'

'As I am really in a hurry for it and cannot spend time in searching about, I suppose I must have it,' said Taboret, 'but I consider the price very high. When will it be ready?'

'By tomorrow evening.'

'Very well, then, be sure it is ready for me by the time I call for it, and, whatever you do, don't make it at all noisy or rough in its ways,' and Taboret swept out of the shop and returned to her home.

Next evening she returned and asked if her job was done.

'I will fetch it, and I am sure you will like it,' said the wizard, leaving the shop as he spoke. Presently he came back, leading by the hand a pretty little girl of about six years old – a little girl so like the Princess Ursula that no one could have told them apart.

'Well,' said Taboret, 'it looks well enough. But are you sure that it's a good piece of workmanship and won't give way anywhere?'

'It's as good a piece of work as ever was done,' said the wizard proudly, striking the child on the back as he spoke. 'Look at it! Examine it all over and see if you find a flaw anywhere. There's not one fairy in twenty who could tell it from the real thing, and no mortal could.'

'It seems to be fairly made,' said Taboret approvingly as she turned the little girl round. 'Now I'll pay you and then will be off,' with which she raised her wand in the air and waved it three times, and there arose a series of strange sounds.

The first was a low tramping, the second shrill and piercing screams, the third voices of wonderful beauty singing a very sorrowful song.

The wizard caught all the sounds and pocketed them at once, and Taboret, without ceremony, picked up the child, took her head downward under her arm and flew away.

At court that night the little Princess had been naughty and had refused to go to bed. It was a long time before her ladies could get her into her crib, and when she was there, she did not really go to sleep, only lay still and pretended till everyone went away; then she got up and stole noiselessly to the window and sat down on the window seat, all curled up in a little bunch, while she looked out wistfully at the moon. She was such a pretty soft little thing, with all her warm bright hair falling over her shoulders, that it would have been hard for most people to be angry with her. She leaned her chin on her tiny white hands, and as she gazed out, the tears rose to her great blue eyes; but, remembering that her ladies would call this naughty, she wiped them hastily away with her nightgown sleeve.

'Ah, moon, pretty bright moon!' she said to herself. 'I wonder if they let you cry when you want to. I think I'd like to go up there and live with you. I'm sure it would be nicer than being here.'

'Would you like to go away with me?' said a voice close beside her, and, looking up, she saw a funny old woman in a red cloak standing near to her. She was not frightened, for the old woman had a kind smile and bright black eyes, though her nose was hooked and her chin long.

'Where would you take me?' said the little Princess, sucking her thumb and staring with all her might.

'I'd take you to the seashore, where you'd be able to play about on the sands, and where you'd have some little boys and girls to play with and no one to tell you not to make a noise.'

'I'll go,' said Ursula, springing up at once.

'Come along,' said the old woman, taking her tenderly in her arms and folding her in her warm red cloak. Then they rose up in the air and flew out of the window, right away over the tops of the houses.

The night was sharp, and Ursula soon fell asleep; but still they kept flying on, on, over hill and dale, for miles and miles, away from the palace, towards the sea.

Far away from the court and the palace, in a tiny fishing village on the sea, was a little hut where a fisherman named Mark lived with his wife and three children. He was a poor man and lived on the fish he caught in his little boat. The children,

Oliver, Philip, and little Bell, were rosy-cheeked and bright-eyed. They played all day long on the shore and shouted till they were hoarse. To this village the fairy bore the still sleeping Ursula and gently placed her on the doorstep of Mark's cottage; then she kissed her cheeks and with one gust blew the door open and disappeared before anyone could come to see who it was.

The fisherman and his wife were sitting quietly within. She was making the children clothes, and he was mending his net, when without any noise the door opened and the cold night air blew in.

'Wife,' said the fisherman, 'just see who's at the door.'

The wife got up and went to the door, and there lay Ursula, still sleeping soundly, in her little white nightdress.

The woman gave a little scream at sight of the child and called to her husband.

'Husband, see, here's a little girl!' and, so saying, she lifted her in her arms and carried her into the cottage. When she was brought into the warmth and light, Ursula awoke and, sitting up, stared about her in fright. She did not cry, as another child might have done, but she trembled very much and was almost too frightened to speak.

Oddly enough, she had forgotten all about her strange flight through the air and could remember nothing to tell the fisherman and his wife but that she was the Princess Ursula; and, on hearing this, the good man and woman thought the poor little girl must be a trifle mad. However, when they examined her little nightdress, made of white fine linen and embroidery, with a crown worked in one corner, they agreed that she must belong to very grand people. They said it would be cruel to send the poor little thing away on such a cold night and they must of course keep till she was claimed. So the woman gave her some warm bread and milk and put her to bed with their own little girl.

In the morning, when the court ladies came to wake Princess
Ursula, they found her sleeping as usual in her little bed,
and little did they think it was not she but a toy Princess
placed there in her stead. Indeed, the ladies were much
pleased, for when they said, 'It is time for Your Royal Highness to arise,' she only answered, 'Certainly,' and let herself
be dressed without another word. And as the time passed
and she was never naughty and scarcely ever spoke, all
said she was vastly improved, and she grew to be a great
favourite.

The ladies all said that the young Princess bid fair to have
the most elegant manners in the country, and the King smiled
and noticed her with pleasure.

In the meantime, in the fisherman's cottage far away, the
real Ursula grew tall and straight as an alder and merry and
light-hearted as a bird.

No one came to claim her, so the good fisherman and his
wife kept her and brought her up among their own little ones.
She played with them on the beach and learned her lessons with
them at school, and her old life had become like a dream she
barely remembered.

But sometimes the mother would take out the little embroidered nightgown and show it to her, and wonder whence
she came and to whom she belonged.

'I don't care who I belong to,' said Ursula. 'They won't
come and take me from you, and that's all I care about.' So she
grew tall and fair, and as she grew, the toy Princess, in her
place at the court, grew too and always was just like her, only
that, whereas Ursula's face was sunburned and her cheeks red
the face of the toy Princess was pale, with only a very slight tint
in her cheeks.

Years passed, and Ursula at the cottage was a tall young
woman, and Ursula at the court was thought to be the most
beautiful there, and everyone admired her manners, though

she never said anything but 'If you please', 'No, thank you', 'Certainly', and 'Just so'.

The King was now an old man, and the fisherman Mark and his wife were grey-headed. Most of their fishing was now done by their eldest son, Oliver, who was their great pride. Ursula waited on them, and cleaned the house, and did the needlework, and was so useful that they could not have done without her. The fairy Taboret had come to the cottage from time to time, unseen by anyone, to see Ursula and, always finding her healthy and merry, was pleased to think of how she had saved her from a dreadful life. But one evening when she paid them a visit, not having been there for some time, she saw something which made her pause and consider. Oliver and Ursula were standing together watching the waves, and Taboret stopped to hear what they said.

'When we are married,' said Oliver softly, 'we will live in that little cottage yonder, so that we can come and see them every day. But that will not be till little Bell is old enough to take your place, for how would my mother do without you?'

'And we had better not tell them', said Ursula, 'that we mean to marry, or else the thought that they are preventing us will make them unhappy.'

When Taboret heard this she became grave and pondered for a long time. At last she flew back to the court to see how things were going on there. She found the King in the middle of a state council. On seeing this, she at once made herself visible, when the King begged her to be seated near him, as he was always glad of her help and advice.

'You find us,' said His Majesty, 'just about to resign our sceptre into younger and more vigorous hands; in fact, we think we are growing too old to reign, and mean to abdicate in favour of our dear daughter, who will reign in our stead.'

'Before you do any such thing,' said Taboret, 'just let me

have a little private conversation with you,' and she led the King into a corner, much to his surprise and alarm.

In about half an hour he returned to the council, looking very white, and with a dreadful expression on his face, whilst he held a handkerchief to his eyes.

'My lords,' he faltered, 'pray pardon our apparently extraordinary behaviour. We have just received a dreadful blow; we hear on authority, which we cannot doubt, that our dear, dear daughter' – here sobs choked his voice and he was almost unable to proceed – 'is – is – in fact not our daughter at all, and only a *sham*.' Here the King sank back in his chair, overpowered with grief, and the fairy Taboret, stepping to the front, told the courtiers the whole story: how she had stolen the real Princess because she feared they were spoiling her, and how she had placed a toy Princess in her place. The courtiers looked from one to another in surprise, but it was evident they did not believe her.

'The Princess is a truly charming young lady,' said the Prime Minister.

'Has Your Majesty any reason to complain of Her Royal Highness's conduct?' asked the old Chancellor.

'None whatever,' sobbed the King. 'She was ever an excellent daughter.'

'Then I don't see', said the Chancellor, 'what reason Your Majesty can have for paying any attention to what this – this person says.'

'If you don't believe me, you old idiots,' cried Taboret, 'call the Princess here, and I'll soon prove my words.'

'By all means,' cried they.

So the King commanded that Her Royal Highness should be summoned.

In a few minutes she came, attended by her ladies. She said nothing, but then she never did speak till she was spoken to. So she entered and stood in the middle of the room silently.

'We have desired that your presence be requested,' the King was beginning, but Taboret without any ceremony advanced towards her and struck her lightly on the head with her wand. In a moment the head rolled on the floor, leaving the body standing motionless as before and showing that it was but an empty shell. 'Just so,' said the head, as it rolled towards the King, and he and the courtiers nearly swooned with fear.

When they were a little recovered, the King spoke again. 'The fairy tells me', he said, 'that there is somewhere a real Princess whom she wishes us to adopt as our daughter. And in the meantime let Her Royal Highness be carefully placed in a cupboard and a general mourning be proclaimed for this dire event.'

So saying, he glanced tenderly at the body and head and turned weeping away.

So it was settled that Taboret was to fetch Princess Ursula and the King and council were to be assembled to meet her.

That evening the fairy flew to Mark's cottage and told them the whole truth about Ursula and that they must part from her.

Loud were their lamentations and great their grief when they heard she must leave them. Poor Ursula herself sobbed bitterly.

'Never mind,' she cried after a time, 'if I am really a great Princess, I will have you all to live with me. I am sure the King, my father, will wish it when he hears how good you have been to me.'

On the appointed day Taboret came for Ursula in a grand coach and four and drove her away to the court. It was a long, long drive, and she stopped on the way and had the Princess dressed in a splendid white silk dress trimmed with gold, and put pearls round her neck and in her hair, that she might appear properly at court.

The King and all the council were assembled with great pomp to greet their new Princess, and all looked grave and anxious. At last the door opened and Taboret appeared, leading the young girl by the hand.

'That is your father!' said she to Ursula, pointing to the King; and on this Ursula, needing no other bidding, ran at once to him and, putting her arms round his neck, gave him a resounding kiss.

His Majesty almost swooned, and all the courtiers shut their eyes and shivered.

'This is really!' said one.

'This is truly!' said another.

'What have I done?' cried Ursula, looking from one to another and seeing that something was wrong but not knowing what. 'Have I kissed the *wrong person*?' On hearing which everyone groaned.

'Come, now,' cried Taboret, 'if you don't like her, I shall take her away to those who do. I'll give you a week, and then I'll come back and see how you're treating her. She's a great deal too good for any of you.' So saying, she flew away on her wand, leaving Ursula to get on with her new friends as best she might. Bur Ursula could not get on with them at all, as she soon began to see.

If she spoke or moved they looked shocked, and at last she was so frightened and troubled by them that she burst into tears, at which they were more shocked still.

'This is indeed a change after our sweet Princess,' said one lady to another.

'Yes, indeed,' was the answer, 'when one remembers how even after her head was struck off she behaved so beautifully and only said, "Just so".'

And all the ladies disliked poor Ursula and soon showed her their dislike. Before the end of the week, when Taboret was to return, she had grown quite thin and pale and seemed afraid of speaking above a whisper.

'Why, what is wrong?' cried Taboret when she returned

and saw how much poor Ursula had changed. 'Don't you like being here? Aren't they kind to you?'

'Take me back, dear Taboret,' cried Ursula, weeping. 'Take me back to Oliver and Philip and Bell. As for these people, I *hate* them.'

And she wept again.

Taboret only smiled and patted her head and then went in to the King and courtiers.

'Now, how is it,' she cried, 'I find the Princess Ursula in tears? And I am sure you are making her unhappy. When you had that bit of wood-and-leather Princess, you could behave well enough to it, but now that you have a real flesh-and-blood woman, you none of you care for her.'

'Our late dear daughter—' began the King, when the fairy interrupted him.

'I do believe,' she said, 'that you would like to have the doll back again. Now I will give you your choice. Which will you have – my Princess Ursula, the real one, or your Princess Ursula, the sham?'

The King sank back into his chair. 'I am not equal to this,' he said. 'Summon the council and let them settle it by vote.' So the council were summoned, and the fairy explained to them why they were wanted.

'Let both Princesses be fetched,' she said; and the toy Princess was brought in with great care from her cupboard, and her head stood on the table beside her, and the real Princess came in with her eyes still red from crying and her bosom heaving.

'I should think there could be no doubt which one would prefer,' said the Prime Minister to the Chancellor.

'I should think not either,' answered the Chancellor.

'Then vote,' said Taboret; and they all voted, and every vote was for the sham Ursula, and not one for the real one. Taboret only laughed.

'You are a pack of sillies and idiots,' she said, 'but you shall have what you want,' and she picked up the head, and with a wave of her wand stuck it on to the body, and it moved round slowly and said, 'Certainly,' just in its old voice; and on hearing this, all the courtiers gave something as like a cheer as they thought polite, whilst the old King could not speak for joy.

'We will', he cried, 'at once make our arrangements for abdicating and leaving the government in the hands of our dear daughter,' and on hearing this the courtiers all applauded again.

But Taboret laughed scornfully and, taking up the real Ursula in her arms, flew back with her to Mark's cottage.

In the evening the city was illuminated and there were great rejoicings at the recovery of the Princess, but Ursula remained in the cottage and married Oliver and lived happily with him for the rest of her life.

PRINCESS SEPTEMBER

W. SOMERSET MAUGHAM

W. Somerset Maugham is a true Englishman, one of the world's best writers of short stories, and a world traveller. In *The Gentleman in the Parlour*, a book about his journeys in the Far East, he introduces this quaint fairy tale. He wrote it while recovering from malaria in a noisy hotel room overlooking the river in Bankgok, Siam. He tells of a Princess and her pet bird, and of the difference between loving and owning a pet.

FIRST the King of Siam had two daughters, and he called them Night and Day. Then he had two more, so he changed the names of the first ones and called the four of them after the seasons, Spring and Autumn, Winter and Summer. But in course of time he had three others, and he changed their names again and called all seven by the days of the week. But when his eighth daughter was born he did not know what to do till he suddenly thought of the months of the year. The Queen said there were only twelve and it confused her to have to remember so many new names, but the King had a methodical mind and when he made it up he never could change it if he tried. He changed the names of all his daughters and called them January, February, March (though of course in Siamese), till he came to the youngest, who was called August, and the next one was called September.

'That only leaves October, November, and December,' said the Queen. 'And after that we shall have to begin all over again.'

'No, we shan't,' said the King, 'because I think twelve daughters are enough for any man, and after the birth of dear little December I shall be reluctantly compelled to cut off your head.'

He cried bitterly when he said this, for he was extremely fond of the Queen. Of course it made the Queen very uneasy, because she knew that it would distress the King very much if he had to cut off her head. And it would not be very nice for her. But it so happened that there was no need for either of them to worry, because September was the last daughter they ever had. The Queen only had sons after that, and they were called by the letters of the alphabet, so there was no cause for anxiety there for a long time, since she had only reached the letter J.

Now the King of Siam's daughters had had their characters permanently embittered by having to change their names in this way, and the older ones, whose names of course had been changed oftener than the others, had their characters more permanently embittered. But September, who had never known what it was to be called anything but September (except of course by her sisters, who, because their characters were embittered, called her all sorts of names), had a very sweet and charming nature.

The King of Siam had a habit which I think might be usefully imitated in Europe. Instead of receiving presents on his birthday he gave them, and it looks as though he liked it, for he used often to say he was sorry he had only been born on one day and so only had one birthday in the year. But in this way he managed in course of time to give away all his wedding presents, and the loyal addresses which the mayors of the cities in Siam presented him with, and all his old crowns which had gone out of fashion. One year on his birthday, not having anything else handy, he gave each of his daughters a beautiful green parrot in a beautiful golden cage. There were nine of them, and on each cage was written the name of the month which was the name of the Princess it belonged to. The nine Princesses were very proud of their parrots, and they spent an hour every day (for, like their father, they were of a methodical turn of mind) in teaching them to talk. Presently all the parrots could say God save the King (in Siamese, which is very difficult), and some of them could say Pretty Polly in no less than seven Oriental languages. But one day when the Princess September went to say good morning to her parrot she found it lying dead at the bottom of its golden cage. She burst into a flood of tears, and nothing that her maids of honour could say comforted her. She cried so much that the maids of honour, not knowing what to do, told the Queen, and the Queen said it was stuff and non-sense and the child had better go to bed without any supper. The maids of honour wanted to go to a party, so they put the Princess September to bed as quickly as they could and left her by herself. And while she lay in her bed, crying still, even though she felt rather hungry, she saw a little bird hop into her room. She took her thumb out of her mouth and sat up. Then the little bird began to sing, and he sang a beautiful song all about the lake in the King's garden, and the willow trees that looked at themselves in the still water, and the goldfish that glided in and out of the branches that were reflected in it. When he had finished, the Princess was not crying any more and she quite forgot that she had had no supper.

'That was a very nice song,' she said.

The little bird gave her a bow, for artistes have naturally good manners and they like to be appreciated.

'Would you care to have me instead of your parrot?' said the little bird. 'It's true that I'm not so pretty to look at, but, on the other hand, I have a much better voice.'

The Princess September clapped her hands with delight, and then the little bird hopped on to the end of her bed and sang her to sleep.

When she awoke next day the little bird was still sitting there, and as she opened her eyes he said, 'Good morning.'

The maids of honour brought in her breakfast, and he ate rice out of her hand, and he had his bath in her saucer. He drank out of it, too. The maids of honour said they didn't think it was very polite to drink one's bath water, but the Princess September said that was the artistic temperament. When he had finished his breakfast he began to sing again so beautifully that the maids of honour were quite surprised, for they had never heard anything like it, and the Princess September was very proud and happy.

'Now I want to show you to my eight sisters,' said the Princess.

She stretched out the first finger of her right hand so that it served as a perch, and the little bird flew down and sat on it. Then, followed by her maids of honour, she went through the palace and called on each of the Princesses in turn, starting with January, for she was mindful of etiquette, and going all the way down to August. And for each of the Princesses the little bird sang a different song. But the parrots could only say God save the King and Pretty Polly. At last she showed the little bird to the King and Queen. They were surprised and delighted.

'I knew I was right to send you to bed without any supper,' said the Queen.

'This bird sings much better than the parrots,' said the King.

'I should have thought you got quite tired of hearing people say "God save the King",' said the Queen. 'I can't think why those girls wanted to teach their parrots to say it too.'

'The sentiment is admirable,' said the King, 'and I never mind how often I hear it. But I do get tired of hearing those parrots say "Pretty Polly".'

'They say it in seven different languages,' said the Princesses.

'I dare say they do,' said the King, 'but it reminds me too much of my councillors. They say the same thing in seven different ways, and it never means anything in any way they say it.'

The Princesses, their characters (as I have already said) being naturally embittered, were vexed at this, and the parrots looked very glum indeed. But the Princess September ran through all the rooms of the palace, singing like a lark, while the little bird flew round and round her, singing like a nightingale, which indeed it was.

Things went on like this for several days, and then the eight Princesses put their heads together. They went to September and sat down in a circle round her, hiding their feet as it is proper for Siamese Princesses to do.

'My poor September,' they said, 'we are so sorry for the death of your beautiful parrot. It must be dreadful for you not to have a pet bird as we have. So we have put all our pocket money together, and we are going to buy you a lovely green and yellow parrot.'

'Thank you for nothing,' said September. (This was not very civil of her, but Siamese Princesses are sometimes a little short with one another.) 'I have a pet bird which sings the most charming songs to me, and I don't know what on earth I should do with a green and yellow parrot.'

January sniffed, then February sniffed, then March sniffed; in fact, all the Princesses sniffed, but in their proper order of precedence. When they had finished September asked them:

'Why do you sniff? Have you all got colds in the head?'

'Well, my dear,' they said, 'it's absurd to talk of *your* bird when the little fellow flies in and out just as he likes.' They looked round the room and raised their eyebrows so high that their foreheads entirely disappeared.

'You'll get dreadful wrinkles,' said September.

'Do you mind our asking where your bird is now?' they said.

'He's gone to pay a visit to his father-in-law,' said the Princess September.

'And what makes you think he'll come back?' asked the Princesses.

'He always does come back,' said September.

'Well, my dear,' said the eight Princesses, 'if you'll take our advice, you won't run any risks like that. If he comes back – and, mind you, if he does you'll be lucky – pop him into the cage and keep him there. That's the only way you can be sure of him.'

'But I like to have him fly about the room,' said the Princess September.

'Safety first,' said her sisters ominously.

They got up and walked out of the room, shaking their heads, and they left September very uneasy. It seemed to her that her little bird was away a long time, and she could not think what he was doing. Something might have happened to him. What with hawks and men with snares, you never knew what trouble he might get into. Besides, he might forget her, or he might take a fancy to somebody else – that would be dreadful; oh, she wished he were safely back again and in the golden cage that stood there empty and ready. For when the maids of honour had buried the dead parrot they had left the cage in its old place.

Suddenly September heard a tweet-tweet just behind her ear, and she saw the little bird sitting on her shoulder. He had come in so quietly and alighted so softly that she had not heard him.

'I wondered what on earth had become of you,' said the Princess.

'I thought you'd wonder that,' said the little bird. 'The fact is I very nearly didn't come back tonight at all. My father-in-law was giving a party, and they all wanted me to stay, but I thought you'd be anxious.'

Under the circumstances, this was a very unfortunate remark for the little bird to make.

September felt her heart go thump, thump against her chest,

and she made up her mind to take no more risks. She put up her hand and took hold of the bird. This he was quite used to – she liked feeling his heart go pit-a-pat, so fast, in the hollow of her hand, and I think he liked the soft warmth of her little hand. So the bird suspected nothing, and he was so surprised when she carried him over to the cage, popped him in, and shut the door on him that for a moment he could think of nothing to say. But in a moment or two he hopped up on the ivory perch and said:

'What is the joke?'

'There's no joke,' said September, 'but some of Mama's cats are prowling about tonight, and I think you're much safer in there.'

'I can't think why the Queen wants to have all those cats,' said the little bird, rather crossly.

'Well, you see, they're very special cats,' said the Princess, 'they have blue eyes and a kink in their tails, and they're a speciality of the Royal Family, if you understand what I mean.'

'Perfectly,' said the little bird, 'but why did you put me in this cage without saying anything about it? I don't think it's the sort of place I like.'

'I shouldn't have slept a wink all night if I hadn't known you were safe.'

'Well, just for this once I don't mind,' said the little bird, 'so long as you let me out in the morning.'

He ate a very good supper and then began to sing. But in the middle of his song he stopped.

'I don't know what is the matter with me,' he said, 'but I don't feel like singing tonight.'

'Very well,' said September, 'go to sleep instead.'

So he put his head under his wing and in a minute was fast asleep. September went to sleep, too. But when the dawn broke she was awakened by the little bird calling her at the top of his voice.

'Wake up, wake up,' he said. 'Open the door of this cage

and let me out. I want to have a good fly while the dew is still on the ground.'

'You're much better off where you are,' said September. 'You have a beautiful golden cage. It was made by the best workman in my papa's kingdom, and my papa was so pleased with it that he cut off his head so that he should never make another.'

'Let me out, let me out,' said the little bird.

'You'll have three meals a day served by my maids of honour; you'll have nothing to worry you from morning till night, and you can sing to your heart's content.'

'Let me out, let me out,' said the little bird. And he tried to slip through the bars of the cage, but of course he couldn't, and he beat against the door, but of course he couldn't open it. Then the eight Princesses came in and looked at him. They told September she was very wise to take their advice. They said he would soon get used to the cage and in a few days would quite forget that he had ever been free. The little bird said nothing at all while they were there, but as soon as they were gone he began to cry again: 'Let me out, let me out.'

'Don't be such an old silly,' said September. 'I've only put you in the cage because I'm so fond of you. *I* know what's good for you much better than you do yourself. Sing me a little song and I'll give you a piece of brown sugar.'

But the little bird stood in the corner of his cage, looking out at the blue sky, and never sang a note. He never sang all day.

'What's the good of sulking?' said September. 'Why don't you sing and forget your troubles?'

'How can I sing?' answered the bird. 'I want to see the trees and the lake and the green rice growing in the fields.'

'If that's all you want, I'll take you for a walk,' said September.

She picked up the cage and went out, and she walked down to the lake round which grew the willow trees, and she stood at the edge of the rice fields that stretched as far as the eye could see.

'I'll take you out every day,' she said. 'I love you and I only want to make you happy.'

'It's not the same thing,' said the little bird. 'The rice fields and the lake and the willow trees look quite different when you see them through the bars of a cage.'

So she brought him home again and gave him his supper. But he wouldn't eat a thing. The Princess was a little anxious at this, and asked her sisters what they thought about it.

'You must be firm,' they said.

'But if he won't eat he'll die,' she answered.

'That would be very ungrateful of him,' they said. 'He must know that you're only thinking of his own good. If he's obstinate and dies, it'll serve him right, and you'll be well rid of him.'

September didn't see how that was going to do *her* very much good, but they were eight to one and all older than she, so she said nothing.

'Perhaps he'll have got used to his cage by tomorrow,' she said.

And next day when she awoke she cried out good morning in a cheerful voice. She got no answer. She jumped out of bed and ran to the cage. She gave a startled cry, for there the little bird lay, at the bottom, on his side, with his eyes closed, and he looked as if he were dead. She opened the door and, putting her hand in, lifted him out. She gave a sob of relief, for she felt that his little heart was beating still.

'Wake up, wake up, little bird,' she said.

She began to cry and her tears fell on the little bird. He opened his eyes and felt that the bars of the cage were no longer round him.

'I cannot sing unless I'm free, and if I cannot sing I die,' he said.

The Princess gave a great sob.

'Then take your freedom,' she said. 'I shut you in a golden cage because I loved you and wanted to have you all to myself. But I never knew it would kill you. Go. Fly away among the trees that are round the lake and fly over the green rice fields. I love you enough to let you be happy in your own way.'

She threw open the window and gently placed the little bird on the sill. He shook himself a little.

'Come and go as you will, little bird,' she said. 'I will never put you in a cage any more.'

'I will come because I love you, little Princess,' said the bird. 'And I will sing you the loveliest songs I know. I shall go far away, but I shall always come back, and I shall never forget you.' He gave himself another shake. 'Good gracious me, how stiff I am,' he said.

Then he opened his wings and flew right away into the blue. But the little Princess burst into tears, for it is very difficult to put the happiness of someone you love before your own, and with her little bird far out of sight she felt on a sudden very lonely. When her sisters knew what had happened, they mocked her and said that the little bird would never return. But he did at last. And he sat on September's shoulder and ate out of her hand and sang her the beautiful songs he had learned while he was flying up and down the fair places of the world. September kept her window open day and night so that the little bird might come into her room whenever he felt inclined, and this was very good for her; so she grew extremely beautiful. And when she was old enough she married the King of Cambodia and was carried all the way to the city in which he lived on a white elephant. But her sisters never slept with their windows open, so they grew extremely ugly as well as disagreeable, and when the time came to marry them off they were given away to the King's councillors with a pound of tea and a Siamese cat.

THE DANCING PRINCESSES

WALTER DE LA MARE

Walter de la Mare was first of all a poet, as you may be able to see by the way he uses words in this story. He was also a great friend of children and rewrote for them many of the famous old tales in his own style. This 'detective story' was first told by the brothers Jakob and Wilhelm Grimm (who were actually language scholars and dictionary makers, and collected fairy tales only as a hobby). It originally ended with the soldier marrying the youngest Princess, but Mr de la Mare gave it a new and more practical ending with a perfect twist.

THERE was a King of old who had twelve daughters. Some of them were fair as swans in spring, some dark as trees on a mountainside, and all were beautiful. And because the King wished to keep their beauty to himself only,

they slept at night in twelve beds in one long stone chamber whose doors were closely barred and bolted.

Yet, in spite of this, as soon as the year came round to May again, and the stars and cold of winter were gone and the world was merry, at morning and every morning the soles of the twelve Princesses' slippers were found to be worn through to the very welts. It was as if they must have been dancing in them all the night long.

News of this being brought to the King, he marvelled. Unless they had wings, how could they have flown out of the palace? There was neither crevice nor cranny in the heavy doors. He spied. He set watch. It made no difference. Brand-new though the Princesses' gold and silver slippers were overnight, they were worn out at morning. He was in rage and despair.

At last this King made a decree. He decreed that anyone who, by waking and watching, by wisdom or magic, should reveal this strange secret, and where and how and when the twelve Princesses' slippers went of nights to get so worn, he should have the hand in marriage of whichever one of the Princesses he chose, and should be made the heir to the throne. As for anyone foolish enough to be so bold as to attempt such a task and fail in it, he should be whipped out of the kingdom and maybe lose his ears into the bargain. But such was the beauty of these Princesses, many a high-born stranger lost not only his heart but his ears also; and the King grew ever more moody and morose.

Now, beyond the walls of the Royal house where lived the twelve Princesses was a forest; and one summer's evening an old soldier who was travelling home from the wars met there, on his way, a beldame with a pig. This old beldame had brought her pig to the forest to feed on the beech mast and truffles, but now, try as she might, she could not prevail upon it to be caught and to return home with her to its sty. She would steal up behind it with its cord in her hand, but as soon as she drew near and all but in touch of it, the pig, that meanwhile had been busily rooting in the cool loose loam, with a flick of its ears and a twinkle of its tail would scamper off out of her reach. It was almost as if its little sharp glass-green eyes could see through the pink shutters of its ears.

The old soldier watched the pig (and the red sunlight was glinting in the young green leaves of the beeches), and at last he said: 'If I may make so bold, Grannie, I know a little secret about pigs. And if, as I take it, you want to catch *that* particular pig, it's yours and welcome.'

The beldame, who had fingers like birds' claws and eyes black as sloes, thanked the old soldier. Fetching out a scrap of some secret root from the bottom of his knapsack, he first slowly turned his back on the pig, then stooped down and, with the bit of root between his teeth, stared earnestly at the pig from between his legs.

Presently, either by reason of the savour of the root or drawn by curiosity, the pig edged closer and closer to the old soldier until at last it actually came nosing and sidling in underneath him, as if under a bridge. Then in a trice the old soldier snatched him up by ear and tail and slipped the noose of the cord fast. The pig squealed like forty demons, but more as if in fun than in real rage.

'There we are, Grannie,' said the old soldier, giving the old beldame her pig, 'and here's a scrap of the root, too. There's no pig all the world over, white, black, or piebald, but after he gets one sniff of it comes for more. *That* I'll warrant you, and I'm sure you're very welcome.'

The beldame, with her pig now safely at the rope's end and the scrap of root between her fingers, thanked the old soldier and asked him of his journey and whither he was going; and it was just as if, with its snout uplifted, its ears drawn forward, the nimble young pig was also listening for his answer.

The old soldier told her he was returning from the wars. 'But as for where *to*, Grannie, or what for, I hardly know. For wife or children have I none, and most of my old friends must have long ago forgotten me. Not that I'm meaning to say, Grannie,' says the soldier, 'that *that* much matters, me being come so far and no turning back. Still, there's just *one* thing I'd like to find out before I go, and that is where the twelve young daughters of the mad old King yonder dance of nights. If I knew that, Grannie, they say I might some day sit on a throne.' With that he burst out laughing, at which the pig, with a twist of its jaws (as though recalling the sweet savour of the root), flung up its three-cornered head and laughed too.

The beldame, eyeing the old soldier closely, said that what

he had asked was not a hard or dangerous matter if only he would promise to do exactly what she told him. The old soldier found *that* easy enough.

'Well,' said the beldame, 'when you come to the palace, you'll be set to watch, and you'll be tempted to sleep. Vow a vow, then, to taste not even a crumb of the sweet cake or sip so much as a sip of the wine the Princesses will bring to you before they go to bed. Wake and watch; then follow where they lead; and here is a cloak which, come fair or foul, will make you invisible.' At this the beldame took a cloak finer than spider silk from out of a small bag or pouch she wore, and gave it him.

'That hide me!' said the soldier. 'Old coat, brass buttons and all?'

'Ay,' said the beldame, and thanked him again for his help; and the pig coughed, and so they parted.

When she was out of sight the old soldier had another look at the magic cloak and thought over what the beldame had told him. Being by nature bold and brave, and having nothing better to do, he went off at once to the King.

The King looked at the old soldier, listened to what he said and then, with a grim smile half hidden under his beard, bade him follow him to a little stone closet hard by the long chamber where the Princesses slept. 'Watch here,' he said, 'and if you can discover this secret, then the reward I have decreed shall be yours. If not –' He glanced up under his brows at the brave old soldier (who had no more fear in his heart than he had money in his pocket), but did not finish his sentence.

A little before nightfall, the old soldier sat himself down on a bench in the stone closet and by the light of a stub of candle began to mend his shoe.

By and by the eldest of the Princesses knocked softly on his door, smiled on him and brought him a cup of wine and a dish of sweet cakes. He thanked her. But as soon as she was gone he dribbled out the wine drip by drip into a hole between the flagstones and made crumbs of the cakes for the mice. Then he lay down and pretended to be asleep. He snored and snored, but even while he snored he was busy with his cobbler's awl boring a little hole for a peephole between the stone of the wall where he lay and the Princesses' room. At midnight all was still.

But hardly had the little owl of midnight called, *Ahoo! Ahoo! Ahoo!* when the old soldier, hearing a gentle stirring in the next room, peeped through the tiny hole he had bored in the wall. His eyes dazzled; a wondrous sight was to be seen. For the Princesses in the filmy silver of the moon were now dressing and attiring themselves in clothes that seemed not of this world but from some strange otherwhere, which they none the less took out of their own coffers and wardrobes. They seemed to be as happy as larks in the morning or like swallows chittering before they fly, laughing and whispering together while they put on these bright garments and made ready. Only one of them, the youngest, had withdrawn herself a little apart and delayed to join them, and now kept silent. Seeing this, her sisters made merry at her and asked her what ailed her.

'The others', she said, 'whom our father set to watch us were young and foolish. But that old soldier has wandered all over the world and has seen many things, and it seems to me he is crafty and wise. That, sisters, is why I say, Beware!'

Still they only laughed at her. 'Crafty and wise, forsooth!' said they. 'Listen to his snoring! He has eaten of our sweet cakes and drunken the spiced wine, and now he will sleep sound till morning.' At this the old soldier, peeping through his little bore hole in the stones, smiled to himself and went on snoring.

When they were all ready to be gone, the eldest of the Princesses clapped her hands. At this signal, and as if by magic, in the middle of the floor one wide flagstone wheeled softly upon its neighbour, disclosing an opening there, and beneath it a narrow winding flight of steps. One by one, according to age, the Princesses followed the eldest down this secret staircase, and the old soldier knew there was no time to be lost.

He flung the old beldame's cloak over his shoulders, and (as she had foretold) instantly of himself there showed not even so much as a shadow. Then, having noiselessly unbarred the door into the Princesses' bedroom, he followed the youngest of them down the stone steps.

It was dark beneath the flagstones, and the old soldier trod clumsily in his heavy shoes. And as he groped down, he stumbled and trod on the hem of the youngest Princess's dress.

'Alas, sisters, a hand is clutching at me!' she called out to her sisters.

'A hand!' mocked the eldest. 'You must have caught your sleeve on a nail!'

On and down they went and out of a narrow corridor at last emerged and came full into the open air, and, following a faint track in the green turf, reached at last a wood where the trees (their bark, branches, twigs, and leaves) were all of silver and softly shimmering in a gentle light that seemed to be neither of sun nor moon nor stars. Anon they came to a second wood, and here the trees shone softly too, but these were of gold. Anon they came to a third wood, and here the trees were in fruit, and the fruits upon them were precious stones – green, blue, amber, and burning orange.

When the Princesses had all passed through this third wood, they broke out upon a hillside, and, looking down from out the leaf-fringed trees, the old soldier saw the calm waters of a lake beyond yellow sands, and drawn up on its strand twelve swan-shaped boats. And there, standing as if in wait beside them, were twelve young men that looked to be Princes. Noble and handsome young men they were.

The Princesses, having hastened down to the strand, greeted these young men one and all, and at once embarked into the twelve swan-shaped boats, the old soldier smuggling himself as gingerly as he could into the boat of the youngest. Then the Princes rowed away softly across the water towards an island that was in the midst of the lake, where was a palace, its windows shining like crystal in the wan light that bathed sky and water.

Only the last of the boats lagged far behind the others, for the old soldier sitting there invisible on the thwart, though little else but bones and sinews, weighed as heavy as a sack of stones in the boat. At last the youngest of the Princes leaned on his oars to recover his breath. 'What', he sighed, 'can be amiss with this boat tonight? It never rowed so heavily.'

The youngest of the Princesses looked askance at him with fear in her eyes, for the boat was atilt with the weight of the old soldier and not trimmed true. Whereupon she turned her small head and looked towards that part of the boat where sat the old soldier, for there it dipped deepest in the water. In so doing, she gazed straight into his eyes, yet perceived nothing but the green water beyond. He smiled at her, and – though she knew not why – she was comforted. 'Maybe,' she said, turning to the Prince again and answering what he had said, 'maybe you are wearied because of the heat of the evening.' And he rowed on.

When they were come to the island and into the palace there, the old soldier could hardly believe his eyes, it was a scene so fair and strange and unearthly. All the long night through, to music of harp and tambour and pipe, the Princesses danced with the Princes. Danced, too, the fountains at play, with an endless singing of birds, trees and flowers blossoming, and no one seemed to weary. But as soon as the scarlet shafts of morning showed beyond these skies, they returned at once to the boats, and the Princesses were soon back safely under the King's roof again, and so fast asleep in their beds that they looked as if they had never stirred or even sighed in them the whole night long. They might be lovely images of stone.

But the old soldier slept like a hare – with one eye open.

When he awoke, which was soon, he began to think over all that he had seen and heard. The longer he pondered on it, the more he was filled with astonishment. Every now and then, as if to make sure of the land of the living, he peeped with his eye through the hole in the wall, for he was almost of a mind to believe that his journey of the night before – the enchanted woods, the lake, the palace, and the music – was nothing more than the make-believe of a dream.

So, being a man of caution, he determined to say nothing at all of what had passed this first night, but to watch again a second night. When dark drew on, he once more dribbled out the spiced wine into the crannies of the stones and crumbled the sweet cakes into morsels for the mice, himself eating nothing but a crust or two of rye bread and a rind of cheese that he had in his haversack.

All happened as before. Midnight came. The Princesses rose up out of their beds, gay and brisk as fish leaping at evening out of their haunts, and soon had made ready and were gone to their trysting place at the lakeside. All was as before.

The old soldier – to make sure even surer – watched for the third night. But this night, as he followed the Princesses, first through the wood where the leaves were of silver, and next where they resembled fine gold, and last where the fruits on the boughs were all of precious stones, he broke off in each a twig. As he did so the third time, the tree faintly sighed, and the youngest Princess heard the tree sigh. Her fears of the first night, far from being lulled and at rest, had only grown sharper. She stayed a moment in the wood, looking back, and cried, 'Sisters! Sisters! We are being watched. We are being followed. I heard this tree sigh, and it was in warning.' But they only laughed at her.

'Sigh, forsooth!' they said. 'So, too, would you, sister, if you were clad in leaves as trees are, and a little wind went through your branches.'

Hearing this, in hope to reassure her, the old soldier softly
wafted the three twigs he carried in the air at a little distance
from the youngest's face. Sweet was the scent of them, and she
smiled. That night, too, for further proof, the old soldier stole
one of the gold drinking cups in the Princes' palace and hid it
away with the twigs in his haversack. Then for the last time he
watched the dancing and listened to the night birds' music and
the noise of the fountains, but, being tired, he sat down and
yawned, for he had no great wish to be young again and was
happy in being himself.

Indeed, as he looked in at the Princesses, fast, fast asleep that
third early morning, their dreamless faces lying waxen and
placid amid the braids of their long hair upon their pillows, he
even pitied them.

That very day he asked to be taken before the King and, when
he was come into his presence, entreated from him a favour.

'Say on!' said the King. The old soldier then besought the
King to promise that if he told the secret thing he had discovered, he would forgive the Princesses all that had gone
before.

'I'd rather', he said, 'be whipped three times round Your
Majesty's kingdom than open my mouth else.'

The King promised. Then the old soldier brought out from
his haversack the three twigs of the trees – the silver and the
gold and the be-gemmed – and the gold cup from the ban-
queting hall; and he told the King all that had befallen him.

On first hearing of this, the King fell into a rage at the
thought of how his daughters had deceived him. But he remembered his promise and was pacified. He remembered, too,
the decree he had made, and sent word that his daughters
should be bidden into his presence. When they were come, the
dark and the fair together, he frowned on them, then turned to
the old soldier: 'Now choose which of these deceivers you will
have for wife, for such was my decree.'

The old soldier, looking at them each in turn, and smiling at the youngest, waved his great hand and said: 'My liege, there is this to be said: Never lived any man high or low that *deserved* a wife as gentle and fair as one of these. But in the place of enchantment I have told of, there were twelve young Princes. Well-spoken and soldierly young men they were; and if it was choosing sons I was, such are the sons I would choose. As for myself, now – if I may be so bold, and if it would be any ease to your Majesty's mind – it being a promise, in a manner of speaking – there's one thing, me having roved the world over all my life, I'm mortal anxious to *know* –' and here he paused.

'Say on,' said the King.

'Why,' replied the old soldier, 'what sort of thing it feels like to sit, even though but for the mite of a moment, on a throne.'

On hearing this, the King grasped his beard and laughed heartily. 'Easily done,' he cried. 'The task is to stay there.'

With his own hand he led the old soldier to the throne, placed his usual crown upon his head, the Royal sceptre in his hand, and with a gesture presented him to all assembled there. There sat the old soldier, with his war-worn face, great bony hands and lean shanks, smiling under the jewelled crown at the company. A merry scene it was.

Then the King earnestly asked the old soldier if he had anything in mind for the future, whereby he might show him his favour. Almost as if by magic, it seemed, the memory of the beldame in the forest came back into the old soldier's head, and he said: 'Well, truth's truth, Your Majesty, and if there *was* such a thing in my mind, it was pigs.'

'Pigs!' cried the King. 'So be it, and so be it, and so be it! Pigs you shall have in plenty,' said he. 'And, by the walls of Jerusalem, of all the animals on God's earth there's none better – fresh, smoked, or salted.'

'Ay, sir,' said the old soldier, 'and even better still with their plump-chapped noddles still on their shoulders and the breath of life in their bodies!'

Then the King sent for his Lord Steward and bade that seven changes of raiment should be prepared for the old soldier, and two mules saddled and bridled, and a fat purse of money put in his hand. Besides these, the King commanded that out of the countless multitude of the Royal pigs should be chosen three score of the comeliest, liveliest, and best, with two lads for their charge.

And when towards sundown a day or two after the old soldier set out from the Royal house into the forest with his laden mules, his pigs and his pig lads, besides the gifts that had been bestowed on him by the twelve noble young Princes and Princesses, he was a glad man indeed. But most he prized a worn-out gold and silver slipper which he had asked of the youngest Princess for a keepsake. This he kept in his knapsack with his magic scrap of root and other such treasures, as if for a charm.

THE PRINCESS OF CHINA

ELEANOR FARJEON

One of England's favourite writers of children's stories, and winner of many prizes, Eleanor Farjeon creates plays, poetry, and stories of very real children as well as unusual fantasy. In this story she shows her fine sense of the fitness of things with a lovely, magical ending.

I WAS nurse to the Princess of China before England was old enough to know it had a name. I had been nurse before that to her mother, the Queen, who was now a widow. The Princess was the tiniest and most enchanting little creature in the world – as light as a butterfly, and as fragile as glass. A silver spoonful of rice made a big meal for her, and when she said, 'Oh, Nanny, I *am* so thirsty!' I would fill my thimble with milk and give it to her to drink; and then she left half of it. I made up her bed in my workbox, and cut my pocket handkerchief in two for a pair of sheets. Her laugh was like the tinkle of a raindrop falling on a glass bell. Really, when I went out walking I was afraid of losing her! So I slipped her into my purse, and left it open, and carried her like that. And as we walked through the streets of Peking, she would peep out of the purse and say, 'What a lot of big people there are in the world, Nanny!' But when we walked in the rice fields and she saw the butterflies at play, she cried, 'Oh, Nanny! Who are all those darling little people, and why do they never come to see me in the palace?'

One day a message came to the Queen of China that the Emperor of Tartary was coming to marry her daughter; and when the Princess had been told the news, she never stopped asking me a string of little questions. 'Where is Tartary,

58

Nanny? Will I like Tartary? Are the people little there, or big? What is the Emperor like? Will I like him? Is he very enormous? Is he nice and tiny? What will he wear?'

I couldn't answer most of her questions, but when she came to the last one, I said, 'He'll wear purple, pet, like every other emperor.'

'Purple!' said she. 'How pretty! Now I shall know him when I see him, my pretty little Purple Emperor!' And the Princess of China clapped her tiny hands.

She grew very excited about her Purple Emperor, and the day he was expected she said suddenly, 'Nanny, I must have a new dress!'

'Why, poppet, you have seven hundred new dresses,' I told her, for hadn't I been kept busy sewing the tiny garments ever since the news came?

'I don't mean *those*,' said she, stamping her foot on my thumbnail, where she was standing at the time. 'I mean a dress that is *really* beautiful enough for a Purple Emperor.'

'Where shall we find it?' I asked her.

'We'll look for it in the rice fields,' said she. So I popped her into my purse, and we set out. The rice fields were as hot as ever, and as full of butterflies, and in them, besides ourselves, was a little Chinese boy, in a blue cotton shirt, chasing the butterflies. Just as we came up, he clapped his two hands together over such a little beauty, as delicate and gay as a flower, and when he parted his hands, the pretty thing fell dead at our feet. The Princess of China wept with rage.

'Make the boy stand still while I pull his hair!' she cried. And the boy had to come close and bend down his head, and she took hold of two of his hairs and pulled them as hard as she could, while he blinked his eyes a little. '*There!*' said she. 'Now go away. I'm never going to look at you again.'

When the boy had gone, the Princess of China said to me, 'Give me the poor little lady, Nanny.' So I picked up the butterfly and gave it to her, and she fondled its soft bloomy wings, and cried a little, and cuddled down inside the purse with it, so deep that I couldn't see her.

'Best let her get over her little fit by herself,' I thought, and looked about for a bit of shade to sit in till she was happy again. And there I rested, watching the butterflies dancing in the heat haze beyond the shadow, and especially one big fine fellow, the handsomest butterfly I had ever seen, who kept hovering in and out of the shadow as though he couldn't keep away from us. At last, as I sat very still, he settled on my purse and remained there quite a long while, moving his long slender feelers this way and that, so that I imagined he was saying something if only I'd had ears tiny enough to hear him.

Whether I dozed or not, who can say? Perhaps I only nodded for a second or so. But when I next looked, I saw the handsome butterfly just spreading his wings to fly, and beside him was another butterfly, much smaller, and of the same gay, delicate sort that the boy had killed. They rose together, their wings touching, and flew out into the sunshine, where they danced awhile, and then disappeared into the haze.

I thought it was now time to return, in case the Emperor of Tartary should be arriving, so I called into my purse, 'Come, poppet, we're going home!' There was no answer, and I supposed she was asleep; so I got up and walked home quietly, not to wake her.

When I reached the palace, the Queen ran out to meet me in a fluster. 'Oh, there you are, Nanny!' said she. 'The Emperor is just entering the city, and we couldn't find you or the Princess anywhere.'

'Here she is, safe in my purse,' I said; and we opened the purse, and it was as empty as an air balloon. We searched every corner of it in vain; and then we ran back together to the rice fields, looking for her in the dust on the way, though I knew she could not have fallen out as I came home without my seeing

it. When we came to the shadow where I had been sitting, we searched the ground thoroughly, but there was not a sign of her. There was nothing but the two butterflies, who had come back and settled first upon my hand and then upon the Queen's. And the little gay one fluttered her wings at me, as though to say, 'See my lovely new dress!' Then it struck me, all of a sudden, and I said to the Queen, who was weeping, 'What sort of a butterfly is this?'

'What a time to ask, Nanny!' wailed the Queen. 'I don't know what sort it is. The big one's a Purple Emperor. But what a time to ask!'

'Dry your eyes,' I said. 'It's useless to look any more. The Princess of China is gone where she'll never come back from.' And I shook the two butterflies off my hand and led the Queen home.

We were met at the palace gates by an excited crowd. The Emperor of Tartary had arrived, and there was no bride to greet him. But as we appeared, the crowd cried, 'Here they are! Here's the Princess's nurse!' and down the steps strode the Emperor of Tartary himself, a great big handsome man in a royal purple mantle. He came straight to the Queen and hugged her saying, 'My Princess! My bride! My beautiful one!'

It took the Queen's breath away, and ours, too. But as soon as she could, she made a sign to me to say nothing, and while the Emperor embraced her again I signed to the crowd. They all understood, and folded their hands in their sleeves, and stood with downcast eyes as the Emperor of Tartary led his bride into the palace. And where was the harm of it? What would he have done with my tiny Princess of China for a bride? He was much better off as he was.

THE MAGIC FISHBONE

CHARLES DICKENS

Perhaps only Charles Dickens, whose long books your great-grand-parents first read as magazine serials, could have written this fairy tale. He himself was the son of a poor clerk 'under Government' in London, and later the father of ten children. Unlike many fathers of his day, he understood perfectly the everday problems of a crowded household. Indeed, Princess Alicia might have been one of his own daughters.

THERE was once a King, and he had a Queen, and he was the manliest of his sex, and she was the loveliest of hers. The King was, in his private profession, under Government. The Queen's father had been a medical man out of town.

They had nineteen children, and were always having more. Seventeen of these children took care of the baby, and Alicia, the eldest, took care of them all. Their ages varied from seven years down to seven months.

Let us now resume our story.

One day the King was going to the office when he stopped at the fishmonger's to buy a pound and a half of salmon not too near the tail, which the Queen (who was a careful housekeeper) has requested him to send home. Mr Pickles, the fishmonger, said, 'Certainly, sir, is there any other article? Good morning.'

The King went on towards the office in a melancholy mood, for quarter day was such a long way off and several of the dear children were growing out of their clothes. He had not pro-ceeded far when Mr Pickles's errand boy came running after him and said, 'Sir, you didn't notice the old lady in our shop.'

'What old lady?' inquired the King. 'I saw none.'

Now, the King had not seen any old lady because this old lady had been invisible to him, though visible to Mr Pickles's boy. Probably because he messed and splashed the water about to that degree, and flopped the pairs of soles down in that violent manner, that, if she had not been visible to him, he would have spoiled her clothes.

Just then the old lady came trotting up. She was dressed in shot silk of the richest quality, smelling of dried lavender.

'King Watkins the First, I believe?' said the old lady.

'Watkins,' replied the King, 'is my name.'

'Papa, if I am not mistaken, of the beautiful Princess Alicia?' said the old lady.

'And of eighteen other darlings,' replied the King.

'Listen. You are going to the office,' said the old lady.

It instantly flashed upon the King that she must be a fairy, or how could she know that?

'You are right,' said the old lady, answering his thoughts, 'I am the good fairy Grandmarina. Attend. When you return home to dinner, politely invite the Princess Alicia to have some of the salmon you bought just now.'

'It may disagree with her,' said the King.

The old lady became so very angry at this absurd idea that the King was quite alarmed and humbly begged her pardon.

'We hear a great deal too much about this thing disagreeing and that thing disagreeing,' said the old lady with the greatest contempt it was possible to express. 'Don't be greedy. I think you want it all yourself.'

The King hung his head under this reproof and said he wouldn't talk about things disagreeing any more.

'Be good, then,' said the fairy Grandmarina, 'and don't! When the beautiful Princess Alicia consents to partake of the salmon – as I think she will – you will find she will leave a fishbone on her plate. Tell her to dry it, and to rub it, and to polish it till it shines like mother-of-pearl, and to take care of it as a present from me.'

'Is that all?' asked the King.

'Don't be impatient, sir,' returned the fairy Grandmarina, scolding him severely. 'Don't catch people short before they have done speaking. Just the way with you grown-up persons. You are always doing it.'

The King again hung his head and said he wouldn't do so any more.

'Be good, then,' said the fairy Grandmarina, 'and don't! Tell the Princess Alicia, with my love, that the fishbone is a magic present which can only be used once; but that it will bring her, that once, whatever she wishes for, PROVIDED SHE WISHES FOR IT AT THE RIGHT TIME. That is the message. Take care of it.'

The King was beginning, 'Might I ask the reason – ?' when the fairy became absolutely furious.

'*Will* you be good, sir?' she exclaimed, stamping her foot on the ground. 'The reason for this, and the reason for that, indeed! You are always wanting the reason. No reason. There! Hoity toity me! I am sick of your grown-up reasons.'

The King was extremely frightened by the old lady's flying into such a passion, and said he was very sorry to have offended her and he wouldn't ask for reasons any more.

'Be good, then,' said the old lady, 'and don't!'

With those words Grandmarina vanished, and the King went on and on and on till he came to the office. There he wrote and wrote and wrote till it was time to go home again. Then he politely invited the Princess Alicia, as the fairy had directed him, to partake of the salmon. And when she had enjoyed it very much, he saw the fishbone on her plate, as the fairy had told him he would, and he delivered the fairy's message, and the Princess Alicia took care to dry the bone, and to rub it, and to polish it till it shone like mother-of-pearl.

And so when the Queen was going to get up in the morning, she said: 'Oh, dear me, dear me, my head, my head!' And then she fainted away.

The Princess Alicia, who happened to be looking in at the chamber door, asking about breakfast, was very much alarmed when she saw her royal mamma in this state, and she rang the bell for Peggy – which was the name of the Lord Chamberlain. But, remembering where the smelling bottle was, she climbed on a chair and got it, and after that she climbed on another chair by the bedside and held the smelling bottle to the Queen's nose, and after that she jumped down and got some water, and after that she jumped up again and wetted the Queen's forehead, and, in short, when the Lord Chamberlain came in, that dear old woman said to the little Princess: 'What a Trot you are! I couldn't have done it better myself!'

But that was not the worst of the good Queen's illness. Oh, no! She was very ill indeed, for a long time. The Princess Alicia kept the seventeen young Princes and Princesses quiet, and dressed and undressed and danced the baby, and made the kettle boil, and heated the soup, and swept the hearth, and poured out the medicine, and nursed the Queen, and did all that ever she could, and was as busy, busy busy, as busy could be. For there were not many servants at that palace, for three reasons: because the King was short of money, because a rise in his office never seemed to come, and because quarter day was so far off that it looked almost as far off and as little as one of the stars.

But on the morning when the Queen fainted away, where was the magic fishbone? Why, there it was in the Princess Alicia's pocket. She had almost taken it out to bring the Queen to life again when she put it back and looked for the smelling bottle.

After the Queen had come out of her swoon that morning, and was dozing, the Princess Alicia hurried upstairs to tell a most particular secret to a most particularly confidential friend of hers, who was a Duchess. People did suppose her to be a doll, but she was really a Duchess, though nobody knew it except the Princess.

This most particular secret was a secret about the magic fishbone, the history of which was well known to the Duchess because the Princess told her everything. The Princess knelt down by the bed on which the Duchess was lying, fully dressed and wide awake, and whispered the secret to her. The Duchess smiled and nodded. People might have supposed that she never smiled and nodded, but she often did, though nobody knew it except the Princess.

Then the Princess Alicia hurried downstairs again to keep watch in the Queen's room. She often kept watch by herself in the Queen's room; but every evening, while the illness lasted, she sat there watching with the King. And every evening the King sat looking at her with a cross look, wondering why she never brought out the magic fishbone. As often as she noticed this, she ran upstairs, whispered the secret to the Duchess over again and said to the Duchess besides: 'They think we children never have a reason or a meaning!' And the Duchess, though the most fashionable Duchess that ever was heard of, winked her eye.

'Alicia,' said the King one evening when she wished him good night.

'Yes, Papa.'

'What is become of the magic fishbone?'

'In my pocket, Papa.'

'I thought you had lost it?'

'Oh, no, Papa!'

'Or forgotten it?'

'No, indeed, Papa.'

And so another time the dreadful little snapping pug dog next door made a rush at one of the young Princes as he stood on the steps coming home from school and terrified him out of his wits, and he put his hand through a pane of glass and bled bled bled. When the seventeen other young Princes and Princesses saw him bleed bleed bleed, they were terrified out of their wits, too, and screamed themselves black in their seventeen faces all at once. But the Princess Alicia put her hands over all their seventeen mouths, one after another, and persuaded them to be quiet because of the sick Queen. And then she put the wounded Prince's hand in a basin of fresh cold water, while they stared with their twice seventeen are thirty-four put down four and carry three eyes, and then she looked in the hand for bits of glass, and there were fortunately no bits of glass there. And then she said to two chubby-legged Princes who were sturdy, though small: 'Bring me in the Royal rag bag. I must snip and stitch and cut and contrive.' So those two young Princes tugged at the Royal rag bag and lugged it in, and the Princess Alicia sat down on the floor with a large pair of scissors and a needle and thread, and snipped and stitched and cut and contrived, and made a bandage and put it on, and it fitted beautifully, and so when it was all done she saw the King her papa looking on by the door.

'Alicia.'

'Yes, Papa.'

'What have you been doing?'

'Snipping, stitching, cutting and contriving, Papa.'

'Where is the magic fishbone?'

'In my pocket, Papa.'

'I thought you had lost it?'

'Oh, no, Papa.'

'Or forgotten it?'

'No, indeed, Papa.'

After that, she ran upstairs to the Duchess and told her what had passed, and told her the secret over again, and the Duchess shook her flaxen curls and laughed with her rosy lips.

Well! and so another time the baby fell under the grate. The seventeen young Princes and Princesses were used to it, for they were almost always falling under the grate or down the stairs, but the baby was not used to it yet, and it gave him a swelled face and a black eye. The way the poor little darling came to tumble was that he slid out of the Princess Alicia's lap just as she was sitting in a great coarse apron that quite smothered her, in front of the kitchen fire, beginning to peel the turnips for the broth for dinner; and the way she came to be doing that was that the King's cook had run away that morning with her own true love, who was a very tall but very tipsy soldier. Then the seventeen young Princes and Princesses, who cried at everything that happened, cried and roared. But the Princess Alicia (who couldn't help crying a little herself) quietly called to them to be still on account of not throwing back the Queen upstairs, who was fast getting well, and said: 'Hold your tongues, you wicked little monkeys, every one of you, while I examine the baby!' Then she examined Baby, and found that he hadn't broken anything, and she held cold iron to his poor dear eye and smoothed his poor dear face, and he presently fell asleep in her arms. Then she said to the seventeen Princes and Princesses: 'I am afraid to lay him down yet, lest he should wake and feel pain. Be good and you shall all be cooks.' They jumped for joy when they heard that, and began making themselves cooks' caps out of old newspapers. So to one she gave the salt box, and to one she gave the barley, and to one she gave the herbs, and to one she gave the turnips, and to one she gave the carrots, and to one she gave the onions, and to one she gave the spice box, till they were all cooks and all running about at work, she sitting in the middle smothered in the great coarse apron, nursing Baby. By and by the broth was done, and the baby woke up smiling like an angel, and was trusted to the sedatest Princess to hold, while the other Princes and Princesses were squeezed into a far-off corner to look at the

Princess Alicia turning out the saucepanful of broth, for fear (as they were always getting into trouble) they should get splashed and scalded. When the broth came tumbling out, steaming beautifully and smelling like a nosegay good to eat, they clapped their hands. That made the baby clap his hands; and that, and his looking as if he had a comic toothache, made all the Princes and Princesses laugh. So the Princess Alicia said: 'Laugh and be good, and after dinner we will make him a nest on the floor in a corner, and he shall sit in his nest and see a dance of eighteen cooks.' That delighted the young Princes and Princesses, and they ate up all the broth, and washed up all the plates and dishes, and cleared away, and pushed the table into a corner, and then they, in their cooks' caps, and the Princess Alicia in the smothering coarse apron that belonged to the cook that had run away with her own true love that was the very tall but very tipsy soldier, danced a dance of eighteen cooks before the angelic baby, who forgot his swelled face and his black eye and crowed with joy.

And so then, once more the Princess Alicia saw King Watkins the First, her father, standing in the doorway looking on, and he said:

'What have you been doing, Alicia?'

'Cooking and contriving, Papa.'

'What else have you been doing, Alicia?'

'Keeping the children light-hearted, Papa.'

'Where is the magic fishbone, Alicia?'

'In my pocket, Papa.'

'I thought you had lost it?'

'Oh, no, Papa.'

'Or forgotten it?'

'No, indeed, Papa.'

The King then sighed so heavily and seemed so low-spirited and sat down so miserably, leaning his head upon his hand and his elbow upon the kitchen table pushed away in the corner, that the seventeen Princes and Princesses crept softly out of the kitchen and left him alone with the Princess Alicia and the angelic baby.

'What is the matter, Papa?'

'I am dreadfully poor, my child.'

'Have you no money at all, Papa?'

'None, my child.'

'Is there no way left of getting any, Papa?'

'No way,' said the King. 'I have tried very hard, and I have tried all ways.'

When she heard those last words, the Princess Alicia began to put her hand into the pocket where she kept the magic fishbone.

'Papa,' said she, 'when we have tried very hard and tried all ways, we must have done our very, very best?'

'No doubt, Alicia.'

'When we have done our very, very best, Papa, and that is not enough, then I think the right time must have come for asking help of others.' This was the very secret connected with the magic fishbone which she had found out for herself from the good fairy Grandmarina's words, and which she had so often whispered to her beautiful and fashionable friend the Duchess.

So she took out of her pocket the magic fishbone that had been dried and rubbed and polished till it shone like mother-of-pearl, and she gave it one little kiss and wished it was quarter day. And immediately it *was* quarter day, and the King's quarter's salary came rattling down the chimney and bounced into the middle of the floor.

But this was not half of what happened, no, not a quarter, for immediately afterwards the good fairy Grandmarina came riding in in a carriage and four (peacocks), with Mr Pickles's boy up behind, dressed in silver and gold, with a cocked hat, powdered hair, pink silk stockings, a jewelled cane, and a nosegay. Down jumped Mr Pickles's boy with his cocked hat in his hand and wonderfully polite (being entirely changed by enchantment) and handed Grandmarina out, and there she stood in her rich shot silk smelling of dried lavender, fanning herself with a sparkling fan.

'Alicia, my dear,' said this charming old fairy, 'how do you do, I hope I see you pretty well, give me a kiss.'

The Princess Alicia embraced her, and then Grandmarina turned to the King and said rather sharply: 'Are you good?'

The King said he hoped so.

'I suppose you know the reason *now* why my god-daughter here,' kissing the Princess again, 'did not apply to the fishbone sooner?' said the fairy.

The King made her a shy bow.

'Ah! But you didn't *then*!' said the fairy.

The King made her a shyer bow.

'Any more reasons to ask for?' said the fairy.

The King said no, and he was very sorry.

'Be good, then,' said the fairy, 'and live happy ever afterwards.'

Then Grandmarina waved her fan, and the Queen came in most splendidly dressed, and the seventeen young Princes and Princesses, no longer grown out of their clothes, came in newly fitted out from top to toe, with tucks in everything to admit of its being let out. After that the fairy tapped the Princess Alicia with her fan, and the smothering coarse apron flew away, and she appeared exquisitely dressed like a little bride, with a wreath of orangeflowers and a silver veil. After that the kitchen dresser changed of itself into a wardrobe, made of beautiful woods and gold and looking glass, which was full of dresses of all sorts, all for her and all exactly fitting her. After that the angelic baby came in, running alone, with his face and eye not a bit the worse but much the better. Then Grandmarina begged to be introduced to the Duchess, and when the Duchess was brought down many compliments passed between them.

A little whispering took place between the fairy and the Duchess, and then the fairy said out loud: 'Yes. I thought she would have told you.' Grandmarina then turned to the King and Queen and said: 'We are going in search of Prince Certainpersonio. The pleasure of your company is requested at church in half an hour precisely.' So she and the Princess Alicia got into the carriage, and Mr Pickles's boy handed in the Duchess, who sat by herself on the opposite seat, and then Mr Pickles's boy put up the steps and got up behind, and the peacocks flew away with their tails spread.

Prince Certainpersonio was sitting by himself, eating barley sugar and waiting to be ninety. When he saw the peacocks followed by the carriage coming in at the window, it immediately occurred to him that something uncommon was going to happen.

'Prince,' said Grandmarina, 'I bring you your bride.'

The moment the fairy said those words, Prince Certainpersonio's face left off being sticky, and his jacket and corduroys changed to peach-bloom velvet, and his hair curled, and a cap and feather flew in like a bird and settled on his head. He got into the carriage by the fairy's invitation, and there he renewed his acquaintance with the Duchess, whom he had seen before.

In the church were the Prince's relations and friends, and the Princess Alicia's relations and friends, and the seventeen Princes and Princesses, and the baby, and a crowd of neighbours. The marriage was beautiful beyond expression. The Duchess was bridesmaid and beheld the ceremony from the pulpit, where she was supported by the cushion of the desk.

Grandmarina gave a magnificent wedding feast afterwards, in which there was everything and more to eat, and everything and more to drink. The wedding cake was delicately ornamented with white satin ribbons, frosted silver and white lilies, and was forty-two yards round.

When Grandmarina had drunk her love to the young couple, and Prince Certainpersonio had made a speech, and everybody had cried Hip, Hip, Hip Hurrah! Grandmarina announced to the King and Queen that in the future there would be eight quarter days in every year, except in leap year, when there would be ten. She turned to Certainpersonio and Alicia and said: 'My dears, you will have thirty-five children, and they will all be good and beautiful. Seventeen of your children will be boys, and eighteen will be girls. The hair of your children will curl naturally. They will never have the measles and will have recovered from the whooping cough before being born.'

'It only remains,' said Grandmarina, 'to make an end of the fishbone.'

So she took it from the hand of the Princess Alicia, and it instantly flew down the throat of the dreadful little snapping pug dog next door and choked him, and he expired in convulsions.

THE BIRTHDAY OF THE INFANTA

OSCAR WILDE

Oscar Wilde's unusual fairy tales with their surprise endings have delighted children for over seventy-five years. Here is one of them, set in the splendour of medieval Spain, in which a spoiled Princess breaks a heart and leaves us to wonder just what kind of person she will grow up to be. Several of the long descriptive passages have been deleted to heighten the drama of the story.

IT WAS the birthday of the Infanta. She was just twelve years of age, and the sun was shining brightly in the gardens of the palace.

Although she was a real Princess and the Infanta of Spain, she had only one birthday every year, just like the children of quite poor people, so it was naturally a matter of great importance to the whole country that she should have a really fine day for the occasion. And a really fine day it certainly was. The tall striped tulips stood straight up upon their stalks, like long rows of soldiers, and looked defiantly across the grass at the roses and said: 'We are quite as splendid as you are now.' The purple butterflies fluttered about with gold dust on their wings, visiting each flower in turn; the little lizards crept out of the crevices of the wall and lay basking in the white glare; and the pomegranates split and cracked with the heat and showed their bleeding red hearts. Even the pale yellow lemons, that hung in such profusion from the mouldering trellis and along the dim arcades, seemed to have caught a richer colour from the wonderful sunlight, and the magnolia trees opened their great globe-like blossoms of folded ivory and filled the air with a sweet heavy perfume.

The little Princess herself walked up and down the terrace with her companions and played at hide and seek round the stone vases and the old moss-grown statues. On ordinary days she was only allowed to play with children of her own rank, so she had always to play alone, but her birthday was an exception, and the King had given orders that she was to invite any of her young friends whom she liked to come and amuse themselves with her. There was a stately grace about these slim Spanish children as they glided about, the boys with their large-plumed hats and short fluttering cloaks, the girls holding up the trains of their long brocaded gowns and shielding the sun from their eyes with huge fans of black and silver. But the Infanta was the most graceful of all, and the most tastefully attired, after the somewhat cumbrous fashion of the day. Her robe was of grey satin, the skirt and the wide puffed sleeves heavily embroidered with silver, and the stiff corset studded with rows of fine pearls. Two tiny slippers with big pink rosettes peeped out beneath her dress as she walked. Pink and pearl was her great gauze fan, and in her hair, which like an aureole of faded gold stood out stiffly round her pale little face, she had a beautiful white rose.

From a window in the palace the sad melancholy King watched them. Behind him stood his brother, Don Pedro of Aragon, whom he hated, and his confessor, the Grand Inquisitor of Granada, sat by his side. Sadder even than usual was the King, for as he looked at the Infanta bowing with childish gravity to the assembling courtiers, or laughing behind her fan at the grim Duchess of Albuquerque, who always accompanied her, he thought of the young Queen, her mother, who but a short time before – so it seemed to him – had come from the gay country of France, and had withered away in the sombre splendour of the Spanish court, dying just six months after the birth of her child, and before she had seen the almonds blossom twice in the orchard.

His whole married life seemed to come back to him today as he watched the Infanta playing on the terrace. She had all the Queen's pretty petulance of manner, the same wilful way of tossing her head, the same proud, curved beautiful mouth, the same wonderful smile – *vrai sourire de France* indeed – as she glanced up now and then at the window or stretched out her little hand for the stately Spanish gentlemen to kiss. But the shrill laughter of the children grated on his ears, and the bright, pitiless sunlight mocked his sorrow, and a dull odour of strange spices, spices such as embalmers use, seemed to taint – or was it fancy? – the clear morning air. He buried his face in his hands, and when the Infanta looked up again the curtains had been drawn and the King had retired.

She made a little *moue* of disappointment and shrugged her shoulders. Surely he might have stayed with her on her birthday. What did the stupid state affairs matter? Or had he gone to that gloomy chapel, where the candles were always burning, and where she was never allowed to enter? How silly of him, when the sun was shining so brightly and everybody was so happy! Besides, he would miss the sham bullfight for which the trumpet was already sounding, to say nothing of the puppet show and the other wonderful things. Her uncle and the Grand Inquisitor were much more sensible. They had come out on the terrace and paid her nice compliments. So she tossed her pretty head and, taking Don Pedro by the hand, she walked slowly down the steps towards a long pavilion of purple silk that had been erected at the end of the garden, the other children following in strict order of precedence, those who had the longest names going first.

A procession of noble boys, fantastically dressed as toreadors, came out to meet her, and the young Count of Tierra-Nueva, a wonderfully handsome lad of about fourteen years of age, uncovering his head with all the grace of a born hidalgo and grandee of Spain, led her solemnly in to a little gilt and ivory chair that was placed on a raised dais above the arena. The children grouped themselves all around, fluttering their big fans and whispering to each other, and Don Pedro and the Grand Inquisitor stood laughing at the entrance. Even the Duchess – the Camerera-Mayor, as she was called – a thin, hard-featured woman with a yellow ruff, did not look quite so bad-tempered as usual, and something like a chill smile flitted across her wrinkled face and twitched her thin, bloodless lips.

It certainly was a marvellous bullfight, and much nicer, the Infanta thought, than the real bullfight that she had been brought to see at Seville on the occasion of the visit of the Duke of Parma to her father. Some of the boys pranced about on richly caparisoned hobbyhorses brandishing long javelins with gay streamers of bright ribands attached to them; others went on foot, waving their scarlet cloaks before the bull and vaulting lightly over the barrier when he charged them; and as for the bull himself, he was just like a live bull, though he was only made of wickerwork and stretched hide and sometimes insisted on running round the arena on his hind legs, which no live bull ever dreams of doing. He made a splendid fight of it, too, and the children got so excited that they stood up upon the benches and waved their lace handkerchiefs and cried out: *Bravo toro! Bravo toro!* just as sensibly as if they had been grown-up people. At last, however, after a prolonged combat, during which several of the hobbyhorses were gored through and through and their riders dismounted, the young Count of Tierra-Neuva brought the bull to his knees and, having obtained permission from the Infanta to give the *coup de grace*, he plunged his wooden sword into the neck of the animal with such violence that the head came right off and disclosed the laughing face of little Monsieur de Lorraine, the son of the French Ambassador at Madrid.

The arena was then cleared amidst much applause, and the

dead hobbyhorses dragged solemnly away by two Moorish pages in yellow and black liveries, and after a short interlude, during which a French posture master performed upon the tight rope, some Italian puppets appeared in the semi-classical tragedy of *Sophonisba* on the stage of a small theatre that had been built up for the purpose. They acted so well, and their gestures were so extremely natural, that at the close of the play the eyes of the Infanta were quite dim with tears. Indeed, some of the children really cried and had to be comforted with sweetmeats, and the Grand Inquisitor himself was so affected that he could not help saying to Don Pedro that it seemed to him intolerable that things made simply out of wood and coloured wax, and worked mechanically by wires, should be so unhappy and meet with such terrible misfortunes.

An African juggler followed, who brought in a large flat basket covered with a red cloth, and, having placed it in the centre of the arena, he took from his turban a curious reed pipe and blew through it. In a few moments the cloth began to move, and as the pipe grew shriller and shriller two green and gold snakes put out their strange wedge-shaped heads and rose slowly up, swaying to and fro with the music as a plant sways in the water. The children, however, were rather frightened at their spotted hoods and quick darting tongues, and were much more pleased when the juggler made a tiny orange tree grow out of the sand and bear pretty white blossoms and clusters of real fruit; and when he took the fan of the little daughter of the Marquess de Las-Torres and changed it into a blue bird that flew all round the pavilion and sang, their delight and amazement knew no bounds.

The solemn minuet, too, performed by the dancing boys from the church of Nuestra Señora Del Pilar, was charming. Everybody was fascinated by the grave dignity with which they moved through the intricate figures of the dance, and by the elaborate grace of their slow gestures and stately bows, and when they had finished their performance and doffed their great plumed hats to the Infanta, she acknowledged their reverence with much courtesy and made a vow that she would send a large wax candle to the shrine of Our Lady of the Pilar in return for the pleasure that she had given her.

A troop of handsome Egyptians – as the gypsies were termed in those days – then advanced into the arena and, sitting down cross-legs in a circle, began to play softly upon their zithers, moving their bodies to the tune and humming, almost below their breath, a low, dreamy air. When they caught sight of Don Pedro they scowled at him, and some of them looked terrified, for only a few weeks before he had had two of their tribe hanged for sorcery in the market place at Seville, but the pretty Infanta charmed them as she leaned back peeping over her fan with her great blue eyes, and they felt sure that one so lovely as she was could never be cruel to anybody.

The funniest part of the whole morning's entertainment was undoubtedly the dancing of the little Dwarf. When he stumbled into the arena, waddling on his crooked legs and wagging his huge, misshapen head from side to side, the children went off into a loud shout of delight, and the Infanta herself laughed so much that the Camerera was obliged to remind her that, although there were many precedents in Spain for a King's daughter weeping before her equals, there were none for a Princess of the blood Royal making so merry before those who were her inferiors in birth. The Dwarf, however, was really quite irresistible, and even at the Spanish court, always noted for its cultivated passion for the horrible, so fantastic a little monster had never been seen. It was his first appearance, too. He had been discovered only the day before, running wild through the forest, by two of the nobles who happened to have been hunting in a remote part of the great cork wood that surrounded the town, and had been carried off by them to the palace as a surprise for the Infanta – his father, who was a poor charcoal burner, being but too well pleased to get rid of so ugly and useless a child. Perhaps the most amusing thing about him was his complete unconsciousness of his own grotesque appearance. Indeed, he seemed quite happy and full of the highest spirits. When the children laughed, he laughed as freely and as joyously as any of them, and at the close of each dance he made them each the funniest of bows, smiling and nodding at them just as if he was really one of themselves and not a little misshapen thing that Nature, in some humorous mood, had fashioned for others to mock at. As for the Infanta, she absolutely fascinated him. He could not keep his eyes off her and seemed to dance for her alone, and when at the close of the performance, remembering how she had seen the great ladies of the court throw bouquets to Caffarelli, the famous Italian treble whom the Pope had sent from his own chapel to Madrid that he might cure the King's melancholy by the sweetness of his voice, she took out of her hair the beautiful white rose and, partly for a jest and partly to tease the Camerera, threw it to him across the arena with her sweetest smile, he took the whole matter quite seriously, and, pressing the flower to his rough, coarse lips he put his hand upon his heart and sank on one knee before her, grinning from ear to ear and with his little bright eyes sparkling with pleasure.

This so upset the gravity of the Infanta that she kept on laughing long after the little Dwarf had run out of the arena, and expressed a desire to her uncle that the dance should be immediately repeated. The Camerera, however, on the plea that the sun was too hot, decided that it would be better that Her Highness should return without delay to the palace, where a wonderful feast had been already prepared for her, including a real birthday cake with her own initials worked all over it in painted sugar and a lovely silver flag waving from the top. The Infanta accordingly rose up with much dignity and, having given orders that the little Dwarf was to dance again for her after the hour of siesta, and conveyed her thanks to the young Count of Tierra-Nueva for his charming reception, she went back to her apartments, the children following in the same order in which they had entered.

Now, when the little Dwarf heard that he was to dance a second time before the Infanta, and by her own express command, he was so proud that he ran out into the garden, kissing the white rose in an absurd ecstasy of pleasure and making the most uncouth and clumsy gestures of delight.

The Infanta had given him the beautiful white rose, and she loved him. How he wished that he had gone back with her! She would have put him on her right hand and smiled at him, and he would have never left her side, but would have made her his playmate and taught her all kinds of delightful tricks. For, though he had never been in a palace before, he knew a great many wonderful things. He could make little cages out of rushes for the grasshoppers to sing in, and fashion the long-jointed bamboo into the pipe that Pan loves to hear. He knew the cry of every bird, and could call the starlings from the treetop or the heron from the mere. He knew the trail of every animal, and could track the hare by its delicate footprints and the boar by the trampled leaves. All the wind dances he knew, the mad dance in red raiment with the autumn, the light dance in blue sandals over the corn, the dance with white snow wreaths in winter, and the blossom dance through the orchards in spring. He knew where the wood pigeons built their nests, and once, when a fowler had snared the parent birds, he had brought up the young ones himself and had built a little dove-cot for them in the cleft of a pollard elm. They were quite tame, and used to feed out of his hands every morning. She would like them, and the rabbits that scurried about in the long fern, and the jays with their steely feathers and black bills, and the hedgehogs that could curl themselves up into prickly balls, and the great wise tortoises that crawled slowly about, shaking their heads and nibbling at the young leaves. Yes, she must certainly come to the forest and play with him. He would give her his own little bed, and would watch outside the window till dawn, to see that the wild horned cattle did not harm her, nor the gaunt wolves creep too near the hut. And at dawn he would tap at the shutters and wake her, and they would go out and dance together all the day long.

But where was she? He asked the white rose, and it made him no answer. The whole palace seemed asleep, and even where the shutters had not been closed, heavy curtains had been drawn across the windows to keep out the glare. He wandered all round looking for some place through which he might gain an entrance, and at last he caught sight of a little private door that was lying open. He slipped through and found himself in a splendid hall, far more splendid, he feared, than the forest, there was so much gilding everywhere, and even the floor was made of great coloured stones, fitted together into a sort of geometrical pattern. But the little Infanta was not there, only some wonderful white statues that looked down on him from their jasper pedestals with sad blank eyes and strangely smiling lips.

At the end of the hall hung a richly embroidered curtain of black velvet, powdered with suns and stars, the King's favourite devices, and broidered on the colour he loved best. Perhaps she was hiding behind that? He would try at any rate.

So he stole quietly across and drew it aside. No; there was only another room, though a prettier room, he thought, than the one he had just left. The walls were hung with a many-figured green arras of needle-wrought tapestry representing a hunt, the work of some Flemish artists who had spent more than seven years in its composition.

The little Dwarf looked in wonder all round him and was half afraid to go on. The strange silent horsemen that galloped so swiftly through the long glades without making any noise seemed to him like those terrible phantoms of whom he had heard the charcoal burners speaking – the Comprachos, who hunt only at night, and if they meet a man, turn him into a hind and chase him. But he thought of the pretty Infanta and took courage. He wanted to find her alone, and to tell her that he, too, loved her. Perhaps she was in the room beyond.

He ran across the soft Moorish carpets and opened the door. No! She was not here either. The room was quite empty.

It was a throne room, used for the reception of foreign ambassadors when the King, which of late had not been often, consented to give them a personal audience. The hangings were of gilt Cordovan leather, and a heavy gilt chandelier with branches for three hundred wax lights hung down from the black and white ceiling. Underneath a great canopy of gold cloth, on which the lions and towers of Castile were broidered in seed pearls, stood the throne itself, covered with a rich pall of black velvet studded with silver tulips and elaborately fringed with silver and pearls.

But the little Dwarf cared nothing for this magnificence. He would not have given his rose for all the pearls on the canopy, nor one white petal of his rose for the throne itself. What he wanted was to see the Infanta before she went down to the pavilion, and to ask her to come away with him when he had finished his dance. Here, in the palace, the air was close and heavy, but in the forest the wind blew free, and the sunlight with wandering hands of gold moved the tremulous leaves aside. Yes: surely she would come if he could only find her! She would come with him to the fair forest, and all day long he would dance for her delight. A smile lit up his eyes at the thought, and he passed into the next room.

Of all the rooms this was the brightest and the most beautiful. The walls were covered with a pink-flowered Lucca damask, patterned with birds and dotted with dainty blossoms

of silver; the furniture was of massive silver, festooned with
florid wreaths and swinging Cupids; in front of the two large
fireplaces stood great screens broidered with parrots and peacocks, and the floor, which was of sea-green onyx, seemed to
stretch far away into the distance. Nor was he alone. Standing
under the shadow of the doorway, at the extreme end of the room,
he saw a little figure watching him. His heart trembled, a cry
of joy broke from his lips and he moved out into the sunlight.
As he did so, the figure moved out also, and he saw it plainly.

The Infanta! It was a monster, the most grotesque monster
he had ever beheld. Not properly shaped, as all other people
were, but hunchbacked and crooked-limbed, with huge lolling
head and mane of black hair. The little Dwarf frowned, and
the monster frowned also. He laughed, and it laughed with him
and held its hands to its sides, just as he himself was doing. He
made it a mocking bow, and it returned him a low reverence.
He went towards it, and it came to meet him, copying each
step that he made and stopping when he stopped himself. He
shouted with amusement and ran forward and reached out his
hand, and the hand of the monster touched his, and it was as
cold as ice. He grew afraid and moved his hand across, and the
monster's hand followed it quickly. He tried to press on, but
something smooth and hard stopped him. The face of the
monster was now close to his own and seemed full of terror. He
brushed his hair off his eyes. It imitated him. He struck at it,
and it returned blow for blow. He loathed it, and it made
hideous faces at him. He drew back, and it retreated.

What is it? He thought for a moment and looked round at
the rest of the room. It was strange, but everything seemed to
have its double in this invisible wall of clear water. Yes, picture
for picture was repeated, and couch for couch. The sleeping
Faun that lay in the alcove by the doorway had its twin brother
that slumbered, and the silver Venus that stood in the sunlight
held out her arms to a Venus as lovely as herself.

Was it Echo? He had called to her once in the valley, and she had answered him word for word. Could she mock the eye as she mocked the voice? Could she make a mimic world just like the real world? Could the shadows of things have colour and life and movement? Could it be that – ?

He started, and, taking from his breast the beautiful white rose, he turned round and kissed it. The monster had a rose of its own, petal for petal the same! It kissed it with like kisses and pressed it to its heart with horrible gestures.

When the truth dawned upon him, he gave a wild cry of despair and fell sobbing to the ground. So it was he who was misshapen and hunchbacked, foul to look at and grotesque. He himself was the monster, and it was at him that all the children had been laughing, and the little Princess who he thought loved him – she, too, had been merely mocking at his ugliness and making merry over his twisted limbs. Why had they not left him in the forest, where there was no mirror to tell him how loathsome he was? Why had his father not killed him, rather than sell him to his shame? The hot tears poured down his cheeks, and he tore the white rose to pieces. The sprawling monster did the same and scattered the faint petals in the air. It grovelled on the ground, and, when he looked at it, it watched him with a face drawn with pain. He crept away, lest he should see it, and covered his eyes with his hands. He crawled, like some wounded thing, into the shadow and lay there moaning.

And at that moment the Infanta herself came in with her companions through the open window, and when they saw the ugly little dwarf lying on the ground and beating the floor with his clenched hands in the most fantastic and exaggerated manner, they went off into shouts of happy laughter, and stood all round him and watched him.

'His dancing was funny,' said the Infanta, 'but his acting is funnier still. Indeed, he is almost as good as the puppets, only,

of course, not quite so natural.' And she fluttered her big fan and applauded.

But the little Dwarf never looked up, and his sobs grew fainter and fainter, and suddenly he gave a curious gasp and clutched his side. And then he fell back again and lay quite still.

'That is capital,' said the Infanta, after a pause, 'but now you must dance for me.'

'Yes,' cried all the children, 'you must get up and dance, for you are as clever as the Barbary apes, and much more ridiculous.'

But the little Dwarf made no answer.

And the Infanta stamped her foot and called out to her uncle, who was walking on the terrace with the Chamberlain, reading some dispatches that had just arrived from Mexico, where the Holy Office had recently been established. 'My funny little

dwarf is sulking,' she cried. 'You must wake him up and tell him to dance for me.'

They smiled at each other and sauntered in, and Don Pedro stooped down and slapped the Dwarf on the cheek with his embroidered glove. 'You must dance,' he said, '*petit monstre.* You must dance. The Infanta of Spain and the Indies wishes to be amused.'

But the little Dwarf never moved.

'A whipping master should be sent for,' said Don Pedro wearily, and he went back to the terrace. But the Chamberlain looked grave, and he knelt beside the little dwarf and put his hand upon his heart. And after a few moments he shrugged his shoulders and rose up and, having made a low bow to the Infanta, he said:

'*Mi bella Princesa,* your funny little dwarf will never dance again. It is a pity, for he is so ugly that he might have made the King smile.'

'But why will he not dance again?' asked the Infanta, laughing.

'Because his heart is broken,' answered the Chamberlain.

And the Infanta frowned, and her dainty rose-leaf lips curled in pretty disdain. 'For the future let those who come to play with me have no hearts,' she cried, and she ran out into the garden.

THE POTTED PRINCESS

RUDYARD KIPLING

Rudyard Kipling, who wrote *The Jungle Books* and *Just So Stories*, spent his boyhood in India and heard the ancient tales of that land from his own Indian nurse, or *ayah*. In this traditional tale from the magical India of flying carpets and rope tricks, Kipling shows us the practical, down-to-earth side too, and points out that the old problem of how to rescue a Princess needs a new and sensible approach.

Now, this is the true tale that was told to Punch, and Judy his sister, by their nurse, in the city of Bombay. They were playing in the veranda, waiting for their mother to come back from her evening drive. The big pink crane, who generally lived by himself at the bottom of the garden because he hated horses and carriages, was with them, too, and the nurse, who was called the ayah, was making him dance by throwing pieces of mud at him. Pink cranes dance very prettily until they grow angry. Then they peck.

This pink crane lost his temper, opened his wings and clattered his beak, and the ayah had to sing a song which never fails to quiet all the cranes in Bombay. It is a very old song, and it says:

> Buggle baita nuddee kinara,
> Toom-toom mushia kaye,
> Nuddee kinara kanta lugga
> Tullaka-tullaka ju jaye.

That means: A crane sat by the riverbank, eating fish *toom-toom*, and a thorn in the riverbank pricked him, and his life went away *tullaka-tullaka* – drop by drop. The ayah and

Punch and Judy always talked Hindustani because they understood it better than English.

'See now,' said Punch, clapping his hands. 'He knows, and he is ashamed. Tullaka-tullaka, ju jaye! Go away!'

'Tullaka-tullaka!' said little Judy, who was five; and the pink crane shut up his beak and went down to the bottom of the garden to the coconut palms and the aloes and the red peppers. Punch followed, shouting 'Tullaka-tullaka!' till the crane hopped over an aloe hedge and Punch got pricked by the spikes. Then he cried, because he was only seven, and because it was so hot that he was wearing very few clothes and the aloes had pricked a great deal of him; and Judy cried, too, because Punch was crying, and she knew that meant something worth crying for.

'Ohoo!' said Punch, looking at both his fat little legs together, 'I am very badly pricked by the very bad aloe. Perhaps I shall die!'

'Punch will die because he has been pricked by the very bad aloe, and then there will be only Judy,' said Judy.

'No,' said Punch, very quickly, putting his legs down. 'Then you will sit up to dinner alone. I will not die; but, ayah, I am very badly pricked. What is good for that?'

The ayah looked down for a minute, just to see that there were two tiny pink scratches on Punch's legs. Then she looked out across the garden to the blue water of Bombay harbour, where the ships are, and said:

'Once upon a time there was a Rajah.' 'Rajah' means King in Hindustani, just as 'Ranee' means Queen.

'Will Punch die, ayah?' said Judy. She, too, had seen the pink scratches, and they seemed very dreadful to her.

'No,' said Punch. 'Ayah is telling a tale. Stop crying, Judy.'

'And the Rajah had a daughter,' said the ayah.

'It is a new tale,' said Punch. 'The last Rajah had a son, and he was turned into a monkey. Hssh!'

The ayah put out her soft brown arm, picked Judy off the matting of the veranda and tucked her into her lap. Punch sat cross-legged close by.

'That Rajah's daughter was very beautiful,' the ayah went on.

'How beautiful? More beautiful than Mama? Then I do not believe this tale,' said Punch.

'She was a fairy Princess, Punch baba, and she was very beautiful indeed; and when she grew up the Rajah her father said that she must marry the best Prince in all India.'

'Where did all these things happen?' said Punch.

'In a big forest near Delhi. So it was told to me,' said the ayah.

'Very good,' said Punch. 'When I am big I will go to Delhi. Tell the tale, ayah.'

'Therefore the King made a talk with his magicians – men with white beards who do *jadoo* (magic), and make snakes come out of baskets, and grow mangoes from little stones, such as you, Punch, and you, Judy baba, have seen. But in those days they did much more wonderful things: they turned men into tigers and elephants. And the magicians counted the stars under which the Princess was born.'

'I – I do not understand this,' said Judy, wriggling on the ayah's lap. Punch did not understand either, but he looked very wise.

The ayah hugged her close. 'How should a baby understand?' she said softly. 'It is in this way. When the stars are in one position when a child is born, it means well. When they are in another position, it means, perhaps, that the child may be sick or ill-tempered, or she may have to travel very far away.'

'Must I travel far away?' said Judy.

'No, no. There were only good little stars in the sky on the night that Judy baba was born – little home-keeping stars that danced up and down, they were so pleased.'

'And I – I! What did the stars do when I was born?' said Punch.

'There was a new star that night. I saw it. A great star with a fiery tale all across the sky. Punch will travel far.'

'That is true. I have been to Nassik in the railway train. Never mind the Princess's stars. What did the magic men do?'

'They consulted the stars, little impatient, and they said that the Princess must be shut up in such a manner that only the very best of all the Princes of India could take her out. So they shut her up, when she was sixteen years old, in a big, deep grain jar of dried clay, with a cover of plaited grass.'

'I have seen them in the Bombay market,' said Judy. 'Was it one of the *very* big kind?' The ayah nodded, and Judy shivered, for her father had once held her up to look into the mouth of just such a grain jar, and it was full of empty darkness.

'How did they feed her?' said Punch.

'She was a fairy. Perhaps she did not want food,' the ayah began.

'All people want food. This is not a true tale. I shall go and beat the crane.' Punch got up on his knees.

'No, no. I have forgotten. There was plenty of food – plantains, red and yellow ones, almond curd, boiled rice and peas, fowl stuffed with raisins and red pepper, and cakes fried in oil with coriander seeds, and sweetmeats of sugar and butter. Is that enough food? So the Princess was shut up in the grain jar, and the Rajah made a proclamation that whoever could take her out should marry her and should govern ten provinces, sitting upon an elephant with tusks of gold. That proclamation was made through all India.'

'We did not hear it, Punch and I,' said Judy. 'Is this a true tale, ayah?'

'It was before Punch was born. It was before even I was born, but so my mother told it to me. And when the proclamation was made, there came to Delhi hundreds and thousands of Princes and Rajahs and great men. The grain jar with the cover of the plaited grass was set in the middle of all, and the Rajah said that he would allow to each man one year in which to make charms and learn great things that would open the grain jar.'

'I do not understand,' said Judy again. She had been looking down the garden for her mother's return, and had lost the thread of the tale.

'The jar was a magic one, and it was to be opened by magic,' said Punch. 'Go on, ayah. I understand.'

The ayah laughed a little. 'Yes, the Rajah's magicians told all the Princes that it was a magic jar, and led them three times round it, muttering under their beards, and bade them come back in a year. So the Princes and the Subdars and the Wazirs and the Maliks rode away east and west and north and south, and consulted the magicians in their fathers' courts, and holy men in caves.'

'Like the holy men I saw at Nassik on the mountain? They were all *nungapunga* (naked), but they showed me their little gods, and I burned stuff that smelled in a pot before them all, and they said I was a Hindu, and – ' Punch stopped, out of breath.

'Yes. Those were the men. Old men smeared with ashes and yellow paint did the Princes consult, and witches and dwarfs that live in caves, and wise tigers and talking horses and learned parrots. They told all these men and all these beasts of the Princess in the grain jar, and the holy men and the wise beasts taught them charms and spells that were very strong magic indeed. Some of the Princes they advised to go out and kill giants and dragons, and cut off their heads. And some of the Princes stayed for a year with the holy men in forests, learning charms that would immediately split open great mountains. There was no charm and no magic that these Princes and Subdars did not learn, for they knew that the

Rajah's magicians were very strong magicians and therefore they needed very, very strong charms to open the grain jar. So they did all these things that I have told, and also cut off the tails of the little devils that live on the sand of the great desert in the north; and at last there were very few dragons and giants left, and poor people could plough without being bewitched any more.

'Only there was one Prince that did not ride away with the others, for he had neither horse nor saddle nor any men to follow him. He was a Prince of low birth, for his father had married the daughter of a potter and he was the son of his mother. So he sat down on the ground, and the little boys of the city driving the cattle to pasture threw mud at him.'

'Ah!' said Punch. 'Mud is nice. Did they hit him?'

'I am telling the tale of the Princess, and if there are so many questions, how can I finish before bedtime? He sat on the ground, and presently his mother, the Ranee, came by, gathering sticks to cook bread, and he told her of the Princess and the grain jar. And she said: "Remember that a pot is a pot, and thou art the son of a potter". Then she went away with those dry sticks, and the Potter Prince waited till the end of the year. Then the Princes returned, as many of them as were left over from the fights that they had fought. They brought with them the terrible cut-off heads of the giants and dragons, so that people fell down with fright; and the tails of all the little devils, bunch by bunch, tied up with string; and the feathers of magic birds; and their holy men and dwarfs and talking beasts came with them. And there were bullock carts full of the locked books of magic incantations and spells. The Rajah appointed a day, and his magicians came, and the grain jar was set in the middle of all, and the Princes began, according to their birth and the age of their families, to open the grain jar by means of their charm work. There were very many Princes, and the charms were very strong, so that as they performed the ceremonies

the lightning ran about the ground as a broken egg runs over the cookhouse floor, and it was thick, dark night, and the people heard the voices of devils and djinns and talking tigers, and saw them running to and fro about the grain jar till the ground shook. But, none the less, the grain jar did not open. And the next day the ground was split up as a log of wood is split, and great rivers flowed up and down the plain, and magic armies with banners walked in circles – so great was the strength of the charms. Snakes, too, crawled round the grain jar and hissed, but, none the less, the jar did not open. When morning came the holes in the ground had closed up, and the rivers were gone away, and there was only the plain. And that was because it was all magic charm work which cannot last.'

'Aha!' said Punch, drawing a deep breath. 'I am glad of that. It was only magic, Judy. Tell the tale, ayah.'

'At the very last, when they were all wearied out and the holy men began to bite their nails with vexation, and the Rajah's magicians laughed, the Potter Prince came into the plain alone, without even one little talking beast or wise bird, and all the people made jokes at him. But he walked to the grain jar and cried "A pot is a pot, and I am the son of a potter!" and he put his two hands upon the grain jar's cover and he lifted it up, and the Princess came out! Then the people said "This is very great magic indeed," and they began to chase the holy men and the talking beasts up and down, meaning to kill them. But the Rajah's magicians said: "This is no magic at all, for we did not put any charm upon the jar. It *was* a common grain jar; and it *is* a common grain jar such as they buy in the bazaar; and a child might have lifted the cover one year ago, or on any day since that day. Ye are too wise, O Princes and Subdars, who rely on holy men and the heads of dead giants and devils' tails, but do not work with your own hands! Ye are too cunning! There was no magic, and now one man has taken it all away from you because he was not afraid. Go home, Princes, or, if ye will, stay to see the wedding. But remember that a pot is a pot".'

There was a long silence at the end of the tale.

'But the charms were very strong,' said Punch doubtfully.

'They were only words, and how could they touch the pot? Could words turn you into a tiger, Punch baba?'

'No. I am Punch.'

'Even so,' said the ayah. 'If the pot had been charmed, a charm would have opened it. But it was a common bazaar pot. What did it know of charms? It opened to a hand on the cover.'

'Oh!' said Punch; and then he began to laugh, and Judy followed his example. 'Now I quite understand. I will tell it to Mama.'

When Mama came back from her drive, the children told her the tale twice over, while she was dressing for dinner; but as they began in the middle and put the beginning first, and then began at the end and put the middle last, she became a little confused.

'Never mind,' said Punch, 'I will show.' And he reached up to the table for the big Eau de Cologne bottle that he was strictly forbidden to touch, and pulled out the stopper and upset half the scent down the front of his dress, shouting, 'A pot is a pot, and I am the son of a potter!'

THE MAGIC HILL

A. A. MILNE

The man who wrote *Winnie the Pooh* wrote other stories for children which are not so well known. Here is one, taken from the little book *A Gallery of Children*, in which a godmother's sweet but bothersome gift is finally used to its best advantage.

Once upon a time there was a King who had seven children. The first three were boys, and he was glad about this because a King likes to have three sons; but when the next three were sons also, he was not so glad, and he wished that one of them had been a daughter. So the Queen said, 'The next shall be a daughter.' And it was, and they decided to call her Daffodil.

When the Princess Daffodil was a month old, the King and Queen gave a great party in the palace for the christening, and the fairy Mumruffin was invited to be godmother to the little Princess.

'She is a good fairy,' said the King to the Queen, 'and I hope

she will give Daffodil something that will be useful to her. Beauty or Wisdom or Riches or –'

'Or Goodness,' said the Queen.

'Or Goodness, as I was about to remark,' said the King.

So you will understand how anxious they were when the fairy Mumruffin looked down at the sleeping Princess in her cradle and waved her wand.

'They have called you Daffodil,' she said, and then she waved her wand again:

> 'Let Daffodil
> The gardens fill.
> Wherever you go
> Flowers shall grow.'

There was a moment's silence while the King tried to think this out.

'What was that?' he whispered to the Queen. 'I didn't quite get that.'

'Wherever she walks flowers are going to grow,' said the Queen. 'I think it's sweet.'

'Oh,' said the King. 'Was that all? She didn't say anything about –'

'No.'

'Oh, well.'

He turned to thank the fairy Mumruffin, but she had already flown away.

It was nearly a year later that the Princess first began to walk, and by this time everybody had forgotten about the fairy's promise. So the King was rather surprised, when he came back from hunting one day, to find that his favourite courtyard, where he used to walk when he was thinking, was covered with flowers.

'What does this mean?' he said sternly to the chief gardener.

'I don't know, Your Majesty,' said the gardener, scratching his head. 'It isn't *my* doing.'

'Then who has done it? Who has been here today?'

'Nobody, Your Majesty, except Her Royal Highness, Princess Daffodil, as I've been told, though how she found her way there, such a baby and all, bless her sweet little –'

'That will do,' said the King. 'You may go.'

For now he remembered. This was what the fairy Mumruffin had promised.

That evening the King and Queen talked the matter over very seriously before they went to bed.

'It is quite clear', said the King, 'that we cannot let Daffodil run about everywhere. That would never do. She must take her walks on the flower beds. She must be carried across all the paths. It will be annoying in a way, but in a way it will be useful. We shall be able to do without most of the gardeners.'

'Yes, dear,' said the Queen.

So Daffodil as she grew up was only allowed to walk on the beds, and the other children were very jealous of her because they were only allowed to walk on the paths; and they thought what fun it would be if only they were allowed to run about on the beds just once. But Daffodil thought what fun it would be if she could run about the paths like other boys and girls.

One day, when she was about five years old, a court doctor came to see her. And when he had looked at her tongue, he said to the Queen:

'Her Royal Highness needs more exercise. She must run about more. She must climb hills and roll down them. She must hop and skip and jump. In short, Your Majesty, although she is a Princess, she must do what other little girls do.'

'Unfortunately,' said the Queen, 'she is not like other little girls.' And she sighed and looked out of the window. And out of the window, at the far end of the garden, she saw a little green hill where no flowers grew. So she turned back to the court doctor and said, 'You are right; she must be as other little girls.'

So she went to the King, and the King gave the Princess Daffodil the little green hill for her very own. And every day the Princess Daffodil played there, and flowers grew; and every evening the girls and boys of the countryside came and picked the flowers.

So they called it the Magic Hill. And from that day onward flowers have always grown on the Magic Hill, and boys and girls have laughed and played and picked them.

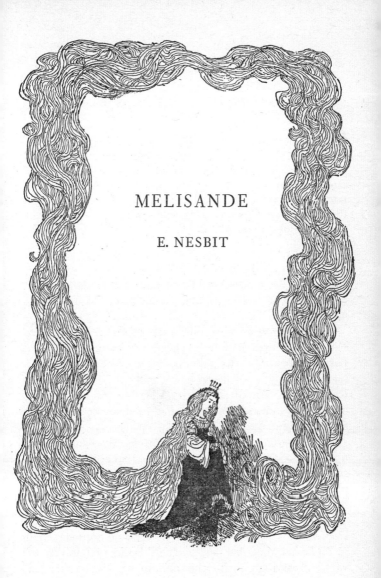

MELISANDE

E. NESBIT

Edith Nesbit probably had more imagination than any other children's writer. Whether she writes of real children, as she does in *The Wouldbegoods*, or of fairy folk, as in *Nine Unlikely Tales*, her characters are always true-to-life and her plots amazing. Here is one of the most unlikely tales, subtitled 'Long and Short Division', about a Princess who couldn't do a thing with her hair and a Prince who could do a lot with his arithmetic.

W HEN the Princess Melisande was born, her mother, the Queen, wished to have a christening party, but the King put his foot down and said he would not have it.

'I've seen too much trouble come of christening parties,' said he. 'However carefully you keep your visiting book, some fairy or other is sure to get left out, and you know what *that* leads to. Why, even in my own family the most shocking things have occurred. The Fairy Malevola was not asked to my great-grandmother's christening – and you know all about the spindle and the hundred years' sleep.'

'Perhaps you're right,' said the Queen. 'My own cousin by marriage forgot some stuffy old fairy or other when she was sending out the cards for her daughter's christening, and the old wretch turned up at the last moment, and the girl drops toads out of her mouth to this day.'

'Just so. And there was that business of the mouse and the kitchenmaids,' said the King. 'We'll have no nonsense about it. I'll be her godfather, and you shall be her godmother, and we won't ask a single fairy; then none of them can be offended.'

'Unless they all are,' said the Queen.

And that was exactly what happened. When the King and Queen and the baby got back from the christening, the parlour-maid met them at the door, and said:

'Please, Your Majesty, several ladies have called. I told them you were not at home, but they all said they'd wait.'

'Are they in the parlour?' asked the Queen.

'I've shown them into the throne room, Your Majesty,' said the parlourmaid. 'You see, there are several of them.'

There were about seven hundred. The great throne room was crammed with fairies, of all ages and of all degrees of beauty and ugliness – good fairies and bad fairies, flower fairies and moon fairies, fairies like spiders and fairies like butterflies – and as the Queen opened the door and began to say how sorry she was to have kept them waiting, they all cried, with one voice: 'Why didn't you ask *me* to your christening party?'

'I haven't had a party,' said the Queen, and she turned to the King and whispered, 'I told you so.' This was her only consolation.

'You've had a christening,' said the fairies, all together.

'I'm very sorry,' said the poor Queen, but Malevola pushed forward and said, 'Hold your tongue!' most rudely.

Malevola is the oldest, as well as the most wicked, of the fairies. She is deservedly unpopular, and has been left out of more christening parties than all the rest of the fairies put together.

'Don't begin to make excuses,' she said, shaking her finger at the Queen. 'That only makes your conduct worse. You know well enough what happens if a fairy is left out of a christening party. We are all going to give our christening presents *now*. As the fairy of highest social position, I shall begin. The Princess shall be bald.'

The Queen nearly fainted as Malevola drew back and another fairy, in a smart bonnet with snakes in it, stepped forward with a rustle of bats' wings. But the King stepped forward, too.

'No, you don't!' said he. 'I wonder at you, ladies, I do indeed. How can you be so unfairylike? Have none of you been to school – have none of you studied the history of your own race? Surely you don't need a poor, ignorant King like me to tell you that this is *no go*?'

'How dare you?' cried the fairy in the bonnet, and the snakes in it quivered as she tossed her head. 'It is my turn, and I say the Princess shall be –'

The King actually put his hand over her mouth.

'Look here,' he said, 'I won't have it. Listen to reason – or you'll be sorry afterwards. A fairy who breaks the traditions of fairy history goes out – you know she does – like the flame of a candle. And all tradition shows that only *one* bad fairy is ever forgotten at a christening party and the good ones are always invited; so either this is not a christening party or else you were all invited except one, and, by her own showing, that was Malevola. It nearly always is. Do I make myself clear?'

Several of the better-class fairies who had been led away by Malevola's influence murmured that there was something in what His Majesty said.

'Try it, if you don't believe me,' said the King. 'Give your nasty gifts to my innocent child – but as sure as you do, out you go, like a candle flame. Now then, will you risk it?'

No one answered, and presently several fairies came up to the Queen and said what a pleasant party it had been, but they really must be going. This example decided the rest. One by one all the fairies said good-bye and thanked the Queen for the delightful afternoon they had spent with her.

'It's been quite too lovely,' said the lady with the snake bonnet. '*Do* ask us again soon, dear Queen. I shall be so *longing* to see you again, and the *dear* baby,' and off she went, with the snake trimming quivering more than ever.

When the very last fairy was gone, the Queen ran to look at the baby – she tore off its Honiton lace cap and burst into tears. For all the baby's downy golden hair came off with the cap, and the Princess Melisande was as bald as an egg.

'Don't cry, my love,' said the King. 'I have a wish lying by, which I've never had occasion to use. My fairy godmother gave it me for a wedding present, but since then I've had nothing to wish for!'

'Thank you, dear,' said the Queen, smiling through her tears.

'I'll keep the wish till baby grows up,' the King went on. 'And then I'll give it to her, and if she likes to wish for hair, she can.'

'Oh, won't you wish for it *now*?' said the Queen, dropping mixed tears and kisses on the baby's round, smooth head.

'No, dearest. She may want something else more when she grows up. And, besides, her hair may grow by itself.'

But it never did. Princess Melisande grew up as beautiful as the sun and as good as gold, but never a hair grew on that little head of hers. The Queen sewed her little caps of green silk, and the Princess's pink and white face looked out of these like a flower peeping out of its bud. And every day as she grew older she grew dearer, and as she grew dearer she grew better, and as she grew more good she grew more beautiful.

Now, when she was grown up, the Queen said to the King:

'My love, our dear daughter is old enough to know what she wants. Let her have the wish.'

So the King wrote to his fairy godmother and sent the letter by a butterfly. He asked if he might hand on to his daughter the wish the fairy had given him for a wedding present.

'I have never had occasion to use it,' said he, 'though it has always made me happy to remember that I had such a thing in the house. The wish is as good as new, and my daughter is now of an age to appreciate so valuable a present.'

To which the fairy replied by return of butterfly:

Dear King,

Pray do whatever you like with my poor little present. I had quite forgotten it, but I am pleased to think that you have treasured my humble keepsake all these years.

Your affectionate godmother,
Fortuna F.

So the King unlocked his gold safe with the several diamond-handled keys that hung at his girdle, and took out the wish and gave it to his daughter.

And Melisande said: 'Father, I will wish all your subjects should be quite happy.'

But they were that already, because the King and Queen were so good. So the wish did not go off.

So then she said: 'Then I wish them all to be good.'

But they were that already, because they were happy. So again the wish hung fire.

Then the Queen said: 'Dearest, for my sake, wish what I tell you.'

'Why, of course I will,' said Melisande. The queen whispered in her ear, and Melisande nodded. Then she said aloud:

'I wish I had golden hair a yard long, and that it would grow an inch every day, and grow twice as fast every time it was cut, and –'

'Stop,' cried the King. And the wish went off, and the next moment the Princess stood smiling at him through a shower of golden hair.

'Oh, how lovely,' said the Queen. 'What a pity you interrupted her, dear; she hadn't finished.'

'What was the end?' asked the King.

'Oh,' said Melisande, 'I was only going to say, "and twice as thick".'

'It's a very good thing you didn't,' said the King. 'You've

done about enough.' For he had a mathematical mind and could do the sums about the grains of wheat on the chessboard, and the nails in the horse's shoes, in his Royal head without any trouble at all.

'Why, what's the matter?' asked the Queen.

'You'll know soon enough,' said the King. 'Come, let's be happy while we may. Give me a kiss, little Melisande, and then go to Nurse and ask her to teach you how to comb your hair.'

'I know,' said Melisande, 'I've often combed Mother's.'

'Your mother has beautiful hair,' said the King, 'but I fancy you will find your own less easy to manage.'

And, indeed, it was so. The Princess's hair began by being a yard long, and it grew an inch every night. If you know anything at all about the simplest sums, you will see that in about five weeks her hair was about two yards long. This is a very inconvenient length. It trails on the floor and sweeps up all the dust, and though in palaces, of course, it is all gold dust, still it is not nice to have it in your hair. And the Princess's hair was growing an inch every night. When it was three yards long, the Princess could not bear it any longer – it was so heavy and so hot – so she borrowed Nurse's cutting-out scissors and cut it all off, and then for a few hours she was comfortable. But the hair went on growing, and now it grew twice as fast as before; so that in thirty-six days it was as long as ever. The poor Princess cried with tiredness; when she couldn't bear it any more, she cut her hair and was comfortable for a very little time. For the hair now grew four times as fast as at first, and in eighteen days it was as long as before and she had to have it cut. Then it grew eight inches a day, and the next time it was cut it grew sixteen inches a day, and then thirty-two inches and sixty-four and a hundred and twenty-eight inches a day, and so on, growing twice as fast after each cutting, till the Princess would go to bed at night with her hair clipped short, and wake up in the morning with yards and yards and yards of golden hair flowing all about the room, so that she could not move without pulling her own hair, and Nurse had to come and cut the hair off before she could get out of bed.

'I wish I was bald again,' sighed poor Melisande, looking at the little green caps she used to wear, and she cried herself to sleep o'nights between the golden billows of the golden hair. But she never let her mother see her cry, because it was the Queen's fault, and Melisande did not want to seem to reproach her.

When first the Princess's hair grew, her mother sent locks of it to all her Royal relations, who had them set in rings and brooches. Later the Queen was able to send enough for bracelets and girdles. But presently so much hair was cut off that they had to burn it. Then when autumn came all the crops failed; it seemed as though all the gold of harvest had gone into the Princess's hair. And there was a famine. Then Melisande said:

'It seems a pity to waste all my hair; it does grow so very fast. Couldn't we stuff things with it, or something, and sell them, to feed the people?'

So the King called a council of merchants, and they sent out samples of the Princess's hair, and soon orders came pouring in; and the Princess's hair became the staple export of that country. They stuffed pillows with it, and they stuffed beds with it. They made ropes of it for sailors to use, and curtains for hanging in Kings' palaces. They made haircloth of it, for hermits and other people who wished to be uncomfy. But it was so soft and silky that it only made them happy and warm, which they did not wish to be. So the hermits gave up wearing it, and, instead, mothers bought it for their little babies, and all well-born infants wore little shirts of Princess hair cloth.

And still the hair grew and grew. And the people were fed and the famine came to an end.

Then the King said: 'It was all very well while the famine

lasted – but now I shall write to my fairy godmother and see if something cannot be done.'

So he wrote and sent the letter by a skylark, and by return of bird came this answer:

'Why not advertise for a competent Prince? Offer the usual reward.'

So the King sent out his heralds all over the world to proclaim that any respectable Prince with proper references should marry the Princess Melisande if he could stop her hair growing.

Then from far and near came trains of Princes anxious to try their luck, and they brought all sorts of nasty things with them in bottles and round wooden boxes. The Princess tried all the remedies, but she did not like any of the Princes, so in her heart she was rather glad that none of the nasty things in bottles and boxes made the least difference to her hair.

The Princess had to sleep in the great throne room now, because no other room was big enough to hold her and her hair. When she woke in the morning the long room would be quite full of her golden hair, packed tight and thick like wood in a barn. And every night when she had had the hair cut close to her head she would sit in her green silk gown by the window and cry, and kiss the little green caps she used to wear, and wish herself bald again.

It was as she sat crying there on Midsummer Eve that she first saw Prince Florizel.

He had come to the palace that evening, but he would not appear in her presence with the dust of travel on him, and she had retired with her hair borne by twenty pages before he had bathed and changed his garments and entered the reception room.

Now he was walking in the garden in the moonlight, and he looked up and she looked down, and for the first time Melisande, looking on a Prince, wished that he might have the power to stop her hair from growing. As for the Prince, he wished many things, and the first was granted him. For he said:

'You are Melisande?'

'And you are Florizel?'

'There are many roses round your window,' said he to her, 'and none down here.'

She threw him one of three white roses she held in her hand. Then he said:

'White rose trees are strong. May I climb up to you?'

'Surely,' said the Princess.

So he climbed up to the window.

'Now,' said he, 'if I can do what your father asks, will you marry me?'

'My father has promised that I shall,' said Melisande, playing with the white roses in her hand.

'Dear Princess,' said he, 'your father's promise is nothing to me. I want yours. Will you give it to me?'

'Yes,' said she, and gave him the second rose.

'I want your hand.'

'Yes,' she said.

'And your heart with it.'

'Yes,' said the Princess, and she gave him the third rose.

'And a kiss to seal the promise.'

'Yes,' said she.

'And a kiss to go with the hand.'

'Yes,' she said.

'And a kiss to bring the heart.'

'Yes,' said the Princess, and she gave him the three kisses.

'Now,' said he, when he had given them back to her, 'tonight do not go to bed. Stay by your window, and I will stay down here in the garden and watch. And when your hair has grown to the filling of your room, call to me, and then do as I tell you.'

'I will,' said the Princess.

So at dewy sunrise the Prince, lying on the turf beside the sun-dial, heard her voice:

'Florizel! Florizel! My hair has grown so long that it is pushing me out of the window.'

'Get out on to the window sill,' said he, 'and twist your hair three times round the great iron hook that is there.'

And she did.

Then the Prince climbed up the rose bush with his naked sword in his teeth, and he took the Princess's hair in his hand about a yard from her head and said:

'Jump!'

The Princess jumped, and screamed, for there she was hanging from the hook by a yard and a half of her bright hair. The Prince tightened his grasp of the hair and drew his sword across it.

Then he let her down gently by her hair till her feet were on the grass, and jumped down after her.

They stayed talking in the garden till all the shadows had crept under their proper trees and the sun-dial said it was breakfast-time.

Then they went in to breakfast, and all the court crowded round to wonder and admire. For the Princess's hair had not grown.

'How did you do it?' asked the King, shaking Florizel warmly by the hand.

'The simplest thing in the world,' said Florizel modestly. 'You have always cut the hair off the Princess. *I* just cut the Princess off the hair.'

'Humph!' said the King, who had a logical mind. And during breakfast he more than once looked anxiously at his daughter. When they got up from breakfast the Princess rose with the rest, but she rose and rose and rose, till it seemed as though there would never be an end of it. The Princess was nine feet high.

'I feared as much,' said the King sadly. 'I wonder what will be the rate of progression. You see,' he said to poor Florizel, 'when we cut the hair off, *it* grows – when we cut the Princess off, *she* grows. I wish you had happened to think of that!'

The Princess went on growing. By dinner-time she was so large that she had to have her dinner brought out into the garden because she was too large to get indoors. But she was too unhappy to be able to eat anything. And she cried so much that there was quite a pool in the garden, and several pages were nearly drowned. So she remembered her *Alice in Wonderland* and stopped crying at once. But she did not stop growing. She grew bigger and bigger and bigger, till she had to go outside the palace gardens and sit on the common, and even that was too small to hold her comfortably, for every hour she grew twice as much as she had done the hour before. And nobody knew what to do, nor where the Princess was to sleep. Fortunately, her clothes had grown with her, or she would have been very cold indeed, and now she sat on the common in her green gown, embroidered with gold, looking like a great hill covered with gorse in flower.

You cannot possibly imagine how large the Princess was growing, and her mother stood wringing her hands on the castle tower, and the Prince Florizel looked on broken-hearted to see his Princess snatched from his arms and turned into a lady as big as a mountain.

The King did not weep or look on. He sat down at once and wrote to his fairy godmother, asking her advice. He sent a weasel with the letter, and by return of weasel he got his own letter back again, marked 'Gone away. Left no address'.

It was now, when the kingdom was plunged into gloom, that a neighbouring King took it into his head to send an invading army against the island where Melisande lived. They came in ships and they landed in great numbers, and Melisande, looking down from her height, saw alien soldiers marching on the sacred soil of her country.

'I don't mind so much now,' said she, 'if I can really be of some use this size.'

And she picked up the army of the enemy in handfuls and double handfuls, and put them back in their ships, and gave a little flip to each transport ship with her finger and thumb, which sent the ships off so fast that they never stopped till they reached their own country, and when they arrived there the whole army to a man said it would rather be court-martialled a hundred times than go near the place again.

Meanwhile Melisande, sitting on the highest hill on the island, felt the land trembling and shivering under her giant feet.

'I do believe I'm getting too heavy,' she said, and jumped off the island into the sea, which was just up to her ankles. Just then a great fleet of warships and gunboats and torpedo boats came in sight, on their way to attack the island.

Melisande could easily have sunk them all with one kick, but she did not like to do this because it might have drowned the sailors, and, besides, it might have swamped the island.

So she simply stooped and picked the island as you would pick a mushroom – for, of course, all islands are supported by a stalk underneath – and carried it away to another part of the world. So that when the warships got to where the island was marked on the map, they found nothing but sea, and a very rough sea it was, because the Princess had churned it all up with her ankles as she walked away through it with the island.

When Melisande reached a suitable place, very sunny and warm, and with no sharks in the water, she set down the island; and the people made it fast with anchors, and then everyone went to bed, thanking the kind fate which had sent them so great a Princess to help them in their need, and calling her the saviour of her country and the bulwark of the nation.

But it is poor work being the nation's bulwark and your country's saviour when you are miles high, and have no one to talk to, and when all you want is to be your humble right size again and to marry your sweetheart. And when it was dark the Princess came close to the island, and looked down, from far up, at her palace and her tower, and cried and cried and cried. It does not matter how much you cry into the sea, it hardly makes any difference, however large you may be. Then when everything was quite dark the Princess looked up at the stars.

'I wonder how soon I shall be big enough to knock my head against them,' said she.

And as she stood star-gazing she heard a whisper right in her ear. A very little whisper, but quite plain.

'Cut off your hair!' it said.

Now, everything the Princess was wearing had grown big along with her, so that now there dangled from her golden girdle a pair of scissors as big as the Malay Peninsula, together with a pincushion the size of the Isle of Wight and a yard measure that would have gone round Australia.

And when she heard the little, little voice, she knew it, small as it was, for the dear voice of Prince Florizel, and she whipped out the scissors from her gold case and snip, snip, snipped all her hair off, and it fell into the sea. The coral insects got hold of it at once and set to work on it, and now they have made it into the biggest coral reef in the world; but that has nothing to do with the story.

Then the voice said, 'Get close to the island,' and the Princess did, but she could not get very close because she was so large, and she looked up again at the stars and they seemed to be much farther off.

Then the voice said, 'Be ready to swim,' and she felt something climb out of her ear and clamber down her arm. The stars got farther and farther away, and next moment the

Princess found herself swimming in the sea, and Prince Florizel swimming beside her.

'I crept on to your hand when you were carrying the island,' he explained, when their feet touched the sand and they walked in through the shallow water, 'and I got into your ear trumpet. You never noticed me because you were so great then.'

'Oh, my dear Prince,' cried Melisande, falling into his arms, 'you have saved me. I am my proper size again.'

So they went home and told the King and Queen. Both were very, very happy, but the King rubbed his chin with his hand and said:

'You've certainly had some fun for your money, young man, but don't you see that we're just where we were before? Why, the child's hair is growing already.'

And indeed it was.

Then once more the King sent a letter to his godmother. He sent it by a flying fish, and by return of fish came the answer:

'Just back from my holidays. Sorry for your troubles. Why not try scales?'

And on this message the whole court pondered for weeks.

But the Prince caused a pair of gold scales to be made, and hung them up in the palace gardens under a big oak tree. And one morning he said to the Princess:

'My darling Melisande, I must really speak seriously to you. We are getting on in life. I am nearly twenty: it is time that we thought of being settled. Will you trust me entirely and get into one of those gold scales?'

So he took her down into the garden and helped her into the scale, and she curled up in it in her green and gold gown, like a little grass mound with buttercups on it.

'And what is going into the other scale?' asked Melisande.

'Your hair,' said Florizel. 'You see, when your hair is cut off you, it grows, and when you are cut off your hair, you grow – oh, my heart's delight, I can never forget how you grew, never! But if, when your hair is no more than you, and you are no more than your hair, I snip the scissors between you and it, then neither you nor your hair can possibly decide which ought to go on growing.'

'Suppose *both* did,' said the poor Princess humbly.

'Impossible,' said the Prince, with a shudder. 'There are limits even to Malevola's malevolence. And, besides, Fortuna said, "Scales." Will you try it?'

'I will do whatever you wish,' said the poor Princess, 'but let me kiss my father and mother once, and Nurse, and you too, my dear, in case I grow large again and can kiss nobody any more.'

So they came one by one and kissed the Princess.

Then the nurse cut off the Princess's hair, and at once it began to grow at a frightful rate.

The King and Queen and nurse busily packed it, as it grew, into the other scale, and gradually the scale went down a little. The Prince stood waiting between the scales with his drawn sword, and just before the two were equal he struck. But during the time his sword took to flash through the air the Princess's hair grew a yard or two, so that at the instant when he struck, the balance was true.

'You are a young man of sound judgement,' said the King, embracing him, while the Queen and the nurse ran to help the Princess out of the gold scale.

The scale full of golden hair bumped down on to the ground as the Princess stepped out of the other one and stood there before those who loved her, laughing and crying with happiness, because she remained her proper size, and her hair was not growing any more.

She kissed her Prince a hundred times, and the very next day they were married. Everyone remarked on the beauty of the bride, and it was noticed that her hair was quite short — only five feet five and a quarter inches long — just down to her pretty ankles. Because the scales had been ten feet ten and a half inches apart, and the Prince, having a straight eye, had cut the golden hair exactly in the middle!

THE PRINCESS AND
THE VAGABONE

RUTH SAWYER

Ruth Sawyer has travelled over most of the world collecting and telling fairy and folk tales. She heard this story from an old seanachie (a highly trained story-teller) sitting by the fire in a cottage in the north of Ireland. It is the basis for Shakespeare's *The Taming of the Shrew*, and the brothers Grimm told it as 'King Thrushbeard'. Miss Sawyer gives it the perfect retelling with just a touch of the Gaelic accent, which turns our word '*vagabond*' into '*vagabone*', and uses '*ye*' instead of '*you*'.

ONCE, in the golden time, when an Irish King sat in every province and plenty covered the land, there lived in Connaught a grand old King with one daughter. She was as tall and slender as the reeds that grow by Lough Erne, and her face was the fairest in seven counties. This was more the pity, for the temper she had did not match

it at all, at all; it was the blackest and ugliest that ever fell to the birthlot of a Princess. She was proud, she was haughty: her tongue had the length and the sharpness of the thorns on a *sidheog* bush; and from the day she was born till long after she was a woman grown she was never heard to say a kind word or known to do a kind deed to a living creature.

As each year passed, the King would think to himself: ''Tis the New Year will see her better.' But it was worse instead of better she grew, until one day the King found himself at the end of his patience, and he groaned aloud as he sat alone, drinking his poteen.

'Faith, another man shall have her for the next eighteen years, for, by my soul, I've had my fill of her!'

So it came about, as I am telling ye, that the King sent word to the nobles of the neighbouring provinces that whosoever would win the consent of his daughter in marriage should have half of his kingdom and the whole of his blessing. On the day that she was eighteen they came: a wonderful procession of Earls, Dukes, Princes, and Kings, riding up to the castle gate, a-courting. The air was filled with the ring of the silver trappings on their horses, and the courtyard was gay with the colours of their bratas and the long cloaks they wore, riding. The King made each welcome according to his rank; and then he sent a serving-man to his daughter, bidding her come and choose her suitor, the time being ripe for her to marry. It was a courteous message that the King sent, but the Princess heard little of it. She flew into the hall on the heels of the serving-man, like a fowl hawk after a bantam cock. Her eyes burned with the anger that was hot in her heart, while she stamped her foot in the King's face until the rafters rang with the noise of it.

'So, ye will be giving me away for the asking – to any one of these blithering fools who has a rag to his back or a castle to his name?'

The King grew crimson at her words. He was ashamed that they should all hear how sharp was her tongue; moreover, he was fearsome lest they should take to their heels and leave him with a shrew on his hands for another eighteen years. He was hard at work piecing together a speech when the Princess strode past him on to the first suitor in the line.

'At any rate, I'll not be choosing ye, ye long-legged corn-crake,' and she gave him a sound kick as she went on to the next. He was a large man with a shaggy beard; and, seeing how the first suitor had fared, he tried a wee bit of a smile on her while his hand went out coaxingly. She saw, and the anger in her grew threefold. She sprang at him, digging the two of her hands deep in his beard, and then she wagged his foolish head back and forth, screaming: 'Take that, and that, and that, ye old whiskered rascal!'

It was a miracle that any beard was left on his face the way that she pulled it. But she left him go free at last and turned to a thin, sharp-faced Prince with a monstrous long nose. The nose took her fancy, and she gave it a tweak, telling the Prince to take himself home before he did any damage with it. The next one she called 'pudding-face' and slapped his fat cheeks until they were purple, and the poor lad groaned with the sting of it.

'Go back to your trough, for I'll not marry a grunter, i' faith,' said she.

She moved swiftly down the line in less time than it takes for the telling. It came to the mind of many of the suitors that they would be doing a wise thing if they betook themselves off before their turn came; as many of them as were not fastened to the floor with fear started away. There happened to be a fat, crooked-legged Prince from Leinster just making for the door when the Princess looked around. In a trice she reached out for the tongs that stood on the hearth near by, and she laid them across his shoulders, sending him spinning into the yard.

'Take that, ye old gander, and good riddance to ye!' she cried after him.

It was then that she saw looking at her a great towering giant of a man; and his eyes burned through hers, deep down into her soul. So great was he that he could have picked her up with a single hand and thrown her after the gander; and she knew it and yet she felt no fear. He was as handsome as Nuada of the Silver Hand; and not a mortal fault could she have found with him, not if she had tried for a hundred years. The two of them stood facing each other, glaring, as if each would spring at the other's throat the next moment; but all the while the Princess was thinking, and thinking how wonderful he was, from the top of his curling black hair down the seven feet of him to the golden clasps on his shoes.

What the man was thinking I cannot be telling. Like a breath of wind on smouldering turf, her liking for him set her anger fierce burning again. She gave him a sound cuff on the ear, then turned, and with a sob in her throat she went flying from the room, the serving-men scattering before her as if she had been a hundred million robbers on a raid.

And the King? Faith, he was dumb with rage. But when he saw the blow that his daughter had given to the finest gentleman in all of Ireland, he went after her as if he had been two hundred million constables on the trail of robbers.

'Ye are a disgrace and a shame to me,' said he, catching up with her and holding firmly to her two hands; 'and, what's more, ye are a disgrace and a blemish to my castle and my kingdom; I'll not keep ye in it a day longer. The first travelling vagabone who comes begging at the door shall have ye for his wife.'

'Will he?' and the Princess tossed her head in the King's face and went to her chamber.

The next morning a poor singing *sthronshuch* came to the castle to sell a song for a penny or a morsel of bread. The song was sweet that he sang, and the Princess listened as Oona, the tirewoman, was winding strands of her long black hair with gold thread.

The gay young wren sang over the moor.
   'I'll build me a nest,' sang he.
''Twill have a thatch and a wee latched door,
   For the wind blows cold from the sea.
And I'll let no one but my true love in,
   For she is the mate for me,'
     Sang the gay young wren.

The wee brown wren by the hedgerow cried,
   'I'll wait for him here,' cried she.
'For the way is far and the world is wide,
   And he might miss the way to me.

Long is the time when the heart is shut,
But I'll open to none save he,'
Sang the wee brown wren.

A strange throb came to the heart of the Princess when the song was done. She pulled her hair free from the hands of the tirewoman.

'Get silver,' she said; 'I would throw it to him.' And when she saw the wonderment grow in Oona's face, she added: 'The song pleased me. Can I not pay for what I like without having ye look at me as if ye feared my wits had flown? Go, get the silver!'

But when she pushed open the grating and leaned far out to throw it, the *sthronshuch* had gone.

For the King had heard the song as well as the Princess. His rage was still with him, and when he saw who it was, he lost no time, but called him quickly inside.

'Ye are as fine a vagabone as I could wish for,' he said. 'Maybe ye are not knowing it, but ye are a bridegroom this day.' And the King went on to tell him the whole tale. The tale being finished, he sent ten strong men to bring the Princess down.

A King's word was law in those days. The vagabone knew this; and, what's more, he knew he must marry the Princess, whether he liked it or no. The vagabone had great height, but he stooped so that it shortened the length of him. His hair was long, and it fell, uncombed and matted, about his shoulders. His brogues were patched, his hose were sadly worn, and with his rags he was the sorriest cut of a man that a maid ever laid her two eyes on. When the Princess came, she was dressed in a gown of gold, with jewels hanging from every thread of it, and her cap was caught with a jewelled brooch. She looked as beautiful as a May morning – with a thundercloud rising back of the hills; and the vagabone held his breath for a moment, watching her. Then he pulled the King gently by the arm.

'I'll not have a wife that looks grander than myself. If I marry your daughter, I must marry her in rags – the same as my own.'

The King agreed 'twas a good idea, and sent for the worst dress of rags in the whole countryside. The rags were fetched, the Princess dressed, the priest brought and the two of them married; and, though she cried and she kicked and she cuffed and she prayed, she was the vagabone's wife – hard and fast.

'Now take her, and good luck go with ye,' said the King. Then his eyes fell on the tongs by the hearth. 'Here, take these along – they may come in handy on the road.'

Out of the castle gate, across the gardens and into the country that lay beyond went the Princess and the vagabone. The sky was blue over their heads and the air was full of spring; each wee creature that passed them on the road seemed bursting with the joy of it. There was naught but anger in the Princess's heart, however; and what was in the heart of the vagabone I cannot be telling. This I know, that he sang the *Song of the Wren* as they went. Often and often the Princess turned back on the road or sat down, swearing she would go no farther; and often and often did she feel the weight of the tongs across her shoulders that day.

At noon the two sat down by the crossroads to rest.

'I am hungry,' said the Princess; 'not a morsel of food have I tasted this day. Ye will go get me some.'

'Not I, my dear,' said the vagabone; 'ye will go beg for yourself.'

'Never,' said the Princess.

'Then ye'll go hungry,' said the vagabone; and that was all. He lighted his pipe and went to sleep with one eye open and the tongs under him.

One, two, three hours passed, and the sun hung low in the sky. The Princess sat there until hunger drove her to her feet. She rose wearily and stumbled on to the road. It might have been the sound of wheels that had started her, I cannot be telling; but as she reached the road a great coach drawn by six black horses came galloping up. The Princess made a sign for it to stop; though she was in rags, yet she was still so beautiful that the coachman drew in the horses and asked her what she was wanting.

'I am near to starving,' and as she spoke the tears started to her eyes, while a new soft note crept into her voice. 'Do ye think your master could spare me a bit of food – or a shilling?' and the hand that had been used to strike went out for the first time to beg.

It was a Prince who rode inside the coach that day, and he heard her. Reaching out a fine, big hamper through the window, he told her she was hearty welcome to whatever she found in it, along with his blessing. But as she put up her arms for it, just, she looked – and saw that the Prince was none other than the fat suitor whose face she had slapped on the day before. Then anger came back to her again, for the shame of begging from him. She emptied the hamper – chicken pasty, jam, currant bread and all – on top of his head, peering through the window, and threw the empty basket at the coachman. Away drove the coach; away ran the Princess and threw herself, sobbing, on the ground, near the vagabone.

''Twas a good dinner that ye lost,' said the vagabone; and that was all. That night they reached a wee scrap of a cabin on the side of a hill. The vagabone climbed the steps and opened the door. 'Here we are at home, my dear,' said he.

'What kind of a home do ye call this?' and the Princess stamped her foot. 'Faith, I'll not live in it.'

'Then ye can live outside; it's all the same to me.' The vagabone went in and closed the door after him; and in a moment he was whistling merrily the song of the wee brown wren.

The Princess sat down on the ground and nursed her poor tired knees. She had walked many a mile that day, with a heavy heart and an empty stomach – two of the worst travelling companions ye can find. The night came down, black as a raven's wing; the dew fell, heavy as rain, wetting the rags and chilling the Princess to the marrow. The wind blew fresh from the sea, and the wolves began their howling in the woods near by; and at last, what with the cold and the fear and the loneliness of it, she could bear it no longer, and she crept softly up to the cabin and went in.

'There's the creepy-stool by the fire, waiting for ye,' said the vagabone; and that was all. But late in the night he lifted her from the chimney corner where she had dropped asleep and laid her gently on the bed, which was freshly made and clean. And he sat by the hearth till dawn, keeping the turf piled high on the fire, so that cold would not waken her. Once he left the hearth; coming to the bedside, he stood a moment to watch her while she slept, and he stooped and kissed the wee pink palm of her hand that lay there like a half-closed lough lily.

Next morning the first thing the Princess asked was where was the breakfast, and where were the servants to wait on her, and where were some decent clothes.

'Your servants are your own two hands, and they will serve ye well when ye teach them how,' was the answer she got.

'I'll have neither breakfast nor clothes if I have to be getting them myself. And shame on ye for treating a wife so,' and the Princess caught up a piggin and threw it at the vagabone.

He jumped clear of it, and it struck the wall behind him. 'Have your own way, my dear,' and he left her, to go out on the bogs and cut turf.

That night the Princess hung the kettle and made stir-about and griddle bread for the two of them.

''Tis the best I have tasted since I was a lad and my mother made the baking,' said the vagabone, and that was all. But often and often his lips touched the braids of her hair as she passed him in the dark; and again he sat through the night, keeping the fire and mending her wee leather brogues, that they might be whole against the morrow.

Next day he brought some sally twigs and showed her how to weave them into creels to sell on coming market day. But the twigs cut her fingers until they bled, and the Princess cried, making the vagabone white with rage. Never had she seen such a rage in another creature. He threw the sally twigs about the cabin, making them whirl and eddy like leaves before an autumn wind; he stamped upon the half-made creel, crushing it to pulp under his feet; and, catching up the table, he tore it to splinters, throwing the fragments into the fire, where they blazed.

'By Saint Patrick, 'tis a bad bargain that ye are! I will take ye this day to the castle in the next county, where I hear they are needing a scullery maid; and there I'll apprentice ye to the King's cook.'

'I will not go,' said the Princess; but even as she spoke, fear showed in her eyes and her knees began shaking in under her.

'Aye, but ye will, my dear,' and the vagabone took up the tongs quietly from the hearth.

For a month the Princess worked in the castle of the King, and all that time she never saw the vagabone. Often and often she said to herself, fiercely, that she was well rid of him; but often, as she sat alone after her work in the cool of the night, she would wish for the song of the wee brown wren, while a new loneliness crept deeper and deeper into her heart.

She worked hard about the kitchen, and as she scrubbed the pots and turned the spit and cleaned the floor with fresh white sand she listened to the wonderful tales the other servants had to tell of the King. They had it that he was the handsomest, aye, and the strongest King in all of Ireland; and every man and child and little creature in his kingdom worshipped him. And after the tales were told the Princess would say to herself: 'If I had not been so proud and free with my tongue, I might have married such a King, and ruled his kingdom with him, learning kindness.'

Now it happened one day that the Princess was told to be unusually spry and careful about her work; and there was a monstrous deal of it to be done: cakes to be iced and puddings to be boiled, fat ducks to be roasted and a whole suckling pig put on the spit to turn.

'What's the meaning of all this?' asked the Princess.

'Ochone, ye poor feeble-minded girl!' and the cook looked at her pityingly. 'Haven't ye heard the King is to be married this day to the fairest Princess in seven counties?'

'Once that was I,' thought the Princess, and she sighed.

'What makes ye sigh?' asked the cook.

'I was wishing, just, that I could be having a peep at her and the King.'

'Faith, that's possible. Do your work well, and maybe I can put ye where ye can see without being seen.'

So it came about, as I am telling ye, at the end of the day, when the feast was ready and the guests come, that the Princess was hidden behind the broidered curtains in the great hall. There, where no one could see her, she watched the hundreds upon hundreds of fair ladies and fine noblemen in their silken dresses and shining coats, all silver and gold, march back and forth across the hall, laughing and talking and making merry among themselves. Then the pipers began to play, and everybody was still. From the farthest end of the hall came two and twenty lads in white and gold; and these were followed by two and twenty pipers in green and gold and two and twenty bowmen in saffron and gold, and, last of all, the King.

A scream, a wee wisp of a cry, broke from the Princess, and she would have fallen had she not caught one of the curtains. For the King was as tall and strong and beautiful as Nuada of the Silver Hand; and from the top of his curling black hair down the seven feet of him to the golden clasps of his shoes he was every whit as handsome as he had been that day when she had cuffed him in her father's castle.

The King heard the cry and stopped the pipers. 'I think,' said he, 'there's a scullery maid behind the curtains. Someone fetch her to me.'

A hundred hands pulled the Princess out; a hundred more pushed her across the hall to the feet of the King and held her there, fearing lest she escape. 'What were ye doing there?' the King asked.

'Looking at ye, and wishing I had the undoing of things I have done,' and the Princess hung her head and sobbed piteously.

'Nay, sweetheart, things are best as they are,' and there came a look into the King's eyes that blinded those watching, so that they turned away and left the two alone.

'Heart of mine,' he went on softly, 'are ye not knowing me?'

'Ye are putting more shame on me because of my evil tongue and the blow my hand gave ye that day.'

'I' faith, it is not so. Look at me.'

Slowly the eyes of the Princess looked into the eyes of the King. For a moment she could not be reading them; she was as a child who pores over a strange tale after the light fades and it has grown too dark to see. But bit by bit the meaning of it came to her, and her heart grew glad with the wonder of it. Out went her arms to him with the cry of loneliness that had been hers so long.

'I never dreamed that it was ye, never once.'

'Can ye ever love and forgive?' asked the King.

'Hush ye!' and the Princess laid her finger on his lips.

The tirewomen were called and she was led away. Her rags were changed for a dress that was spun from gold and woven with pearls, and her beauty shone about her like a great light. They were married again that night, for none of the guests were knowing of that first wedding long ago.

Late o' that night a singing *sthronshuch* came under the Princess's window, and very softly the words of his song came to her:

> The gay young wren sang over the moor.
> 'I'll build me a nest,' sang he.
> ''Twill have a thatch and a wee latched door,
> For the wind blows cold from the sea.
> And I'll let no one but my true love in,
> For she is the mate for me.'
> Sang the gay young wren.
>
> The wee brown wren by the hedgerow cried,
> 'I'll wait for him here,' cried she.
> 'For the way is far and the world is wide,
> And he might miss the way to me.
> Long is the time when the heart is shut,
> But I'll open to none save he,'
> Sang the wee brown wren.

The grating opened slowly; the Princess leaned far out, her eyes like stars in the night, and when she spoke there was naught but gentleness and love in her voice.

'Here is the silver I would have thrown ye on a day long gone by. Shall I throw it now, or will ye come for it?'

And that was how a Princess of Connaught was won by a King who was a vagabone.

THE PRINCESS

ARCHIBALD MARSHALL

Archibald Marshall's stories were written for both children and grown-ups, and he called them *Simple Stories*, perhaps because they are always short and have very little punctuation. They first appeared in *Punch*. This one tells of a Prince who *didn't* want to marry the Princess, and what the Princess did about it.

ONCE there was a Prince who went to his father and said I want to marry Rose.

His father said who is Rose? and he said she is the girl I want to marry.

And his father said why do you want to marry her? and he said because I like the shape of her face.

So his father said well you can't, and he said why not?

And his father said because I have just arranged for you to marry a very nice Princess.

And he said what Princess?

His father said I forget her name but she is the daughter of a King who is very rich and I owe him some money.

So the Prince went away very sad, and when he had gone the King clapped his hands together and his caitiff came to him and touched the ground with his forehead and said Salaam.

And the King said bring me my hookah, and when he had brought him his hookah he said do you know a girl called Rose? and he said yes.

And the King said well put her in a dungeon.

So the caitiff touched the ground with his forehead again and said Amen and went out.

Well that evening the Prince went to Rose's house and asked for her, and her mother said she is not here, and he said where is she? and she said I don't know.

So the Prince was very sad, and that night at the banquet he could not eat any of the rich and delicate viands but drank a little iced sherbet flavoured with pineapple because his father was looking at him.

And after the banquet he went out into the garden which was very lovely and had a million roses in it and a great many bulbuls which was what they called nightingales. And they were all singing and it was very lovely, but the Prince said I would rather hear Rose's bulbul than any of those, I think I will go indoors.

Now Rose had a tame nightingale which she had taught to speak, and directly the Prince had said I think I will go indoors he heard a voice, and it said Rose is here.

So he knew it was Rose's nightingale and he said where? And it said in the dungeon.

So the Prince rescued Rose out of the dungeon and he put her on his swift Arab steed and fled with her into the desert.

Well they came to a small oasis where there was a well and a palm tree with some dates on it, but when they had eaten all the dates they were still very hungry, and the Prince said if somebody doesn't come soon we shall die.

And Rose was very brave and she said oh well never mind.

Well just as they were going to die they saw a caravan coming with plenty of camels and dromedaries, and it was the caravan of the Princess who was coming to marry the Prince.

The Princess was a little old but she was very nice. The Prince did not tell her who he was at first but he told her that he wanted to marry Rose and his father wouldn't let him so he had fled with her into the desert.

And the Princess said quite right too and you shall marry Rose, I will see to it.

The Prince said thank you, and the Princess said I like weddings and used to play at them when I was a little girl, and I have brought my private clergyman with me and if you don't mind my religion being a little different he can marry you now if you like, I expect it will count but if not you can be done again when you get home.

So the Prince was married to Rose and the Princess gave him a lovely kaboosh with rubies and emeralds for a wedding present, and she gave Rose a shawl to go on with and said she would give her something more when her camels were un-packed.

So the next day the Prince told the Princess who he was, and she said oh well it can't be helped now and you are a little young for me, perhaps I can marry your father, it would be a pity not to marry somebody as I have come so far.

So the Princess married the King, because his wife was dead and anyhow he was allowed by his religion to have as many wives as he liked if he didn't have too many and was kind to all of them.

And he forgave the Prince for marrying Rose, and he said she is very nice and I don't think you could have done better.

THE LIGHT PRINCESS

GEORGE MACDONALD

George MacDonald wrote *At the Back of the North Wind*, two books about a Princess, and many stories. He was a minister and a professor of literature at London University. His stories are full of meaning, but he never lets a 'lesson' interfere with the wonderful magic and humour of his plots. Here is one of his finest works, especially abridged to fit into this collection, which tells of a Princess who floats in the air and laughs at sorrow because she has no gravity at all.

O NCE upon a time, so long ago that I have quite forgotten the date, there lived a King and Queen who had no children.

And the King said to himself, 'All the Queens of my acquaintance have children, some three, some seven, and some as many as twelve; and my Queen has not one. I feel ill-used.' So he made up his mind to be cross with his wife about it. But she bore it all like a good patient Queen, as she was. Then the King grew very cross indeed. But the Queen pretended to take it all as a joke, and a very good one, too.

'Why don't you have any daughters, at least?' said he. 'I don't say *sons*; that might be too much to expect.'

'I am sure, dear King, I am very sorry,' said the Queen.

'So you ought to be,' retorted the King; 'you are not going to make a virtue of *that*, surely.'

But he was not an ill-tempered King, and in any matter of less moment would have let the Queen have her own way with all his heart. This, however, was an affair of state.

The Queen smiled.

'You must have patience with a lady, you know, dear King,' said she.

She was, indeed, a very nice Queen, and heartily sorry that she could not oblige the King immediately.

The King tried to have patience, but he succeeded very badly. It was more than he deserved, therefore, when, at last, the Queen gave him a daughter – as lovely a little Princess as ever cried.

When the day drew near when the infant must be christened, the King wrote all the invitations with his own hand. Of course somebody was forgotten.

Now, it does not generally matter if somebody *is* forgotten, only you must mind who. Unfortunately, the King forgot without intending to forget; and so the chance fell upon the Princess Makemnoit, which was awkward. For the Princess was the King's own sister; and he ought not to have forgotten her. But she had made herself so disagreeable to the old King, their father, that he had forgotten her in making his will; and so it was no wonder that her brother forgot her in writing his invitations. But what made it highly imprudent in the King to forget her was – that she was a witch; she beat all the wicked fairies in wickedness. Therefore, after waiting and waiting in vain for an invitation, she made up her mind at last to go without one and make the whole family miserable.

So she put on her best gown, went to the palace, was kindly received by the happy monarch, who forgot that he had forgotten her, and took her place in the procession to the Royal chapel. When they were all gathered about the font, she contrived to get next to it and threw something into the water; after which she maintained a very respectful demeanour till the water was applied to the child's face. But at that moment she turned round in her place three times and muttered the following words, loud enough for those beside her to hear:

'Light of spirit, by my charms,
Light of body, every part,
Never weary human arms –
Only crush thy parents' heart!'

They all thought she had lost her wits and was repeating some foolish nursery rhyme; but a shudder went through the whole of them notwithstanding. The baby, on the contrary, began to laugh and crow; while the nurse gave a start and a smothered cry, for she thought she was struck with paralysis: she could not feel the baby in her arms. But she clasped it tight and said nothing.

The mischief was done.

Her atrocious aunt had deprived the child of all her gravity. If you ask me how this was effected, I answer, 'In the easiest way in the world. She had only to destroy gravitation.' For the Princess was a philosopher, and knew all the *ins* and *outs* of the laws of gravitation as well as the *ins* and *outs* of her boot-lace. And, being a witch as well, she could abrogate those laws in a moment.

The first awkwardness that resulted from this unhappy privation was that the moment the nurse began to float the baby up and down, she flew from her arms towards the ceiling. There she remained, horizontal as when she left her nurse's arms, kicking and laughing amazingly. The nurse in terror flew to the bell and begged the footman who answered it to bring up the house steps directly. Trembling in every limb, she climbed upon the steps and had to stand upon the very top and reach up before she could catch the floating tail of the baby's long clothes.

When the strange fact came to be known, there was a terrible commotion in the palace. The occasion of its discovery by the King was naturally a repetition of the nurse's experience. Astonished that he felt no weight when the child was laid in his arms, he began to wave her up and – not down, for she slowly ascended to the ceiling as before. Turning to the Queen, who was just as horror-struck as himself, the King said, gasping, staring, and stammering,

'She *can't* be ours, Queen!'

'I am sure she is ours,' answered she. 'But we ought to have taken better care of her at the christening. People who were never invited ought not to have been present.'

'Oh, oh!' said the King, tapping his forehead with his forefinger. 'I have it all. I've found her out. Don't you see it, Queen? Princess Makemnoit has bewitched her.'

'That's just what I say,' answered the Queen.

One fine summer day, a month after these her first adventures, during which time she had been very carefully watched, the Princess was lying on the bed in the Queen's own chamber, fast asleep. One of the windows was open, for it was noon, and the day so sultry that the little girl was wrapped in nothing less ethereal than slumber itself. The Queen came into the room and, not observing that the baby was on the bed, opened another window. A frolicsome fairy wind, which had been watching for a chance of mischief, rushed in at the one window and, taking its way over the bed where the child was lying, caught her up and, rolling and floating her along like a piece of flue or a dandelion seed, carried her with it through the opposite window and away. The Queen went downstairs, quite ignorant of the loss she had herself occasioned.

When the nurse returned, she supposed that Her Majesty had carried her off, and, dreading a scolding, delayed making inquiry about her. But, hearing nothing, she grew uneasy and went at length to the Queen's boudoir, where she found Her Majesty.

'Please, Your Majesty, shall I take the baby?' said she.

'Where is she?' asked the Queen. Then she saw that something was amiss and fell down in a faint. The nurse rushed about the palace, screaming, 'My baby! My baby!'

In a moment the palace was like a beehive in a garden; and

in one minute more the Queen was brought to herself by a great shout and a clapping of hands. They had found the Princess fast asleep under a rose bush, to which the elvish little wind puff had carried her, finishing its mischief by shaking a shower of red rose leaves all over the little white sleeper. Startled by the noise the servants made, she woke and, furious with glee, scattered the rose leaves in all directions, like a shower of spray in the sunset.

She was watched more carefully after this, no doubt; yet it would be endless to relate all the odd incidents resulting from this peculiarity of the young Princess.

One day, after breakfast, the King went into his counting-house and counted out his money.

The operation gave him no pleasure.

'To think,' said he to himself, 'that every one of these gold sovereigns weighs a quarter of an ounce and my real, live, flesh-and-blood Princess weighs nothing at all!'

And he hated his gold sovereigns as they lay with a broad smile of self-satisfaction all over their yellow faces.

The Queen was in the parlour, eating bread and honey. But at the second mouthful she burst out crying and could not swallow it. The King heard her sobbing. Glad of anybody, but especially of his Queen, to quarrel with, he clashed his gold sovereigns into his money-box, clapped his crown on his head, and rushed into the parlour.

'What is all this about?' exclaimed he. 'What are you crying for, Queen?'

'I can't eat it,' said the Queen, looking ruefully at the honey pot.

'No wonder!' retorted the King. 'You've just eaten your breakfast – two turkey eggs and three anchovies.'

'Oh, that's not it!' sobbed Her Majesty. 'It's my child, my child!'

'Well, what's the matter with your child? She's neither up

the chimney nor down the draw well. Just hear her laughing.'

Yet the King could not help a sigh, which he tried to turn into a cough, saying.

'It is a good thing to be light-hearted, I am sure, whether she be ours or not.'

'It is a bad thing to be light-headed,' answered the Queen, looking with prophetic soul far into the future.

''Tis a good thing to be light-handed,' said the King.

''Tis a bad thing to be light-fingered,' answered the Queen.

''Tis a good thing to be light-footed,' said the King.

''Tis a bad thing –' began the Queen; but the King interrupted her.

'In fact,' said he, with the tone of one who concludes an argument in which he has had only imaginary opponents and in which, therefore, he has come off triumphant 'In fact, it is a good thing altogether to be light-bodied.'

'But it is a bad thing altogether to be light-minded,' retorted the Queen, who was beginning to lose her temper.

This last answer quite discomfited His Majesty, who turned on his heel and started off to his counting-house again. But he was not half-way towards it when he turned upon his heel, and rejoined the Queen. She looked so rueful that the King took her in his arms; and they sat down to consult.

'Can you bear this?' said the King.

'No, I can't,' said the Queen.

'Well, what's to be done?' said the King.

'I'm sure I don't know,' said the Queen. 'But might you not try an apology?'

'To my old sister, I suppose you mean?' said the King.

'Yes,' said the Queen.

'Well, I don't mind,' said the King.

So he went the next morning to the House of the Princess and, making a very humble apology, begged her to undo the spell. But the Princess declared, with a grave face, that she knew nothing at all about it. Her eyes, however, shone pink, which was a sign that she was happy. She advised the King and Queen to have patience and to mend their ways. The King returned disconsolate.

Meantime, notwithstanding awkward occurrences and griefs that she brought upon her parents, the little Princess laughed and grew – not fat, but plump and tall. She reached the age of seventeen without having fallen into any worse scrape than a chimney, by rescuing her from which a little bird-nesting urchin got fame and a black face. Nor, thoughtless as she was, had she committed anything worse than laughter at everybody and everything that came in her way. When she was told, for the sake of experiment, that General Clanrunfort was cut to pieces with all his troops, she laughed; when she heard that the enemy was on his way to besiege her papa's capital, she laughed hugely; but when she was told that the city would certainly be abandoned to the mercy of the enemy's soldiery – why, then she laughed immoderately. She never could be brought to see the serious side of anything. When her mother cried, she said,

'What queer faces Mama makes! And she squeezes water out of her cheeks! Funny Mama!'

And when her papa stormed at her, she laughed and danced round and round him, clapping her hands and crying,

'Do it again, Papa. Do it again! It's such fun! Dear funny Papa!'

And if he tried to catch her, she glided from him in an instant, not in the least afraid of him, but thinking it part of the game not to be caught. With one push of her foot, she would be floating in the air above his head; or she would go dancing backward and forward and sideways, like a great butterfly. It happened several times, when her father and mother were holding a consultation about her in private, that they were interrupted by vainly repressed outbursts of laughter over their heads and, looking up with indignation, saw her floating at full length in the air above them, whence she regarded them with the most comical appreciation of the position.

She laughed like the very spirit of fun; only in her laugh there was something missing. What it was, I find myself unable to describe. I think it was a certain tone, depending upon the possibility of sorrow – *morbidezza*, perhaps. She never smiled.

After a long avoidance of the painful subject, the King and Queen resolved to hold a council of three upon it; and so they sent for the Princess. In she came, sliding and flitting and gliding from one piece of furniture to another, and put herself at last in an armchair in a sitting posture. Whether she could be said *to sit*, seeing she received no support from the seat of the chair, I do not pretend to determine.

'My dear child,' said the King, 'you must be aware by this time that you are not exactly like other people.'

'Oh, you dear funny Papa! I have got a nose, and two eyes, and all the rest. So have you. So has Mama.'

'Now be serious, my dear, for once,' said the Queen.

'No, thank you, Mama; I had rather not.'

'Would you not like to be able to walk like other people?' said the King.

'No, indeed, I should think not. You only crawl. You are such slow-coaches!'

'How do you feel, my child?' he resumed, after a pause of discomfiture.

'Quite well, thank you.'

'I mean, what do you feel like?'

'Like nothing at all, that I know of.'

'You must feel like something.'

'I feel like a Princess with such a funny Papa, and such a dear pet of a Queen-mama!'

'Now, really!' began the Queen; but the Princess interrupted her.

'Oh, yes,' she added, 'I remember. I have a curious feeling sometimes, as if I were the only person that had any sense in the whole world.'

She had been trying to behave herself with dignity; but now she burst into a violent fit of laughter, threw herself backward over the chair and went rolling about the floor in an ecstasy of enjoyment. The King picked her up easier than one does a down quilt and replaced her in her former relation to the chair. The exact preposition expressing this relation I do not happen to know.

'Is there nothing you wish for?' resumed the King, who had learned by this time that it was quite useless to be angry with her. 'Oh, you dear Papa! — yes,' answered she.

'What is it, my darling?'

'I have been longing for it – oh, such a time! Ever since last night.'

'Tell me what it is.'

'Will you promise to let me have it?'

The King was on the point of saying *Yes*, but the wiser Queen checked him with a single motion of her head.

'Tell me what it is first,' said he.

'No, no. Promise first.'

'I dare not. What is it?'

'Mind, I hold you to your promise. It is – to be tied to the end of a string – a very long string indeed, and be flown like a kite. Oh, such fun! I would rain rose water, and hail sugar plums, and snow whipped cream, and – and – and –'

A fit of laughter checked her, and she would have been off again over the floor, had not the King started up and caught her just in time. Seeing that nothing but talk could be got out of her he rang the bell, and sent her away with two of her ladies-in-waiting.

Perhaps the best thing for the Princess would have been to fall in love. But how a Princess who had no gravity could fall into anything is a difficulty – perhaps *the* difficulty. As for her own feelings on the subject, she did not even know that there was such a beehive of honey and stings to be fallen into. But now I come to mention another curious fact about her.

The palace was built on the shore of the loveliest lake in the world; and the Princess loved this lake more than father or mother. The root of this preference no doubt, although the Princess did not recognize it as such, was that the moment she got into it she recovered the natural right of which she had been so wickedly deprived – namely, gravity. Whether this was owing to the fact that water had been employed as the means of conveying the injury, I do not know. But it is certain that she could swim and dive like the duck that her old nurse said she was.

Indeed, the passion of her life was to get into the water, and she was always the better behaved and the more beautiful the more she had of it. Summer and winter it was quite the same; only she could not stay so long in the water when they had to break the ice to let her in. Any day, from morning till evening in summer, she might be descried – a streak of white in the blue water – lying as still as the shadow of a cloud or shooting along like a dolphin, disappearing and coming up again far off, just where one did not expect her. She would have been in the lake of a night, too, if she could have had her way; for the balcony of her window overhung a deep pool in it, and through a shallow reedy passage she could have swum out into the wide wet water, and no one would have been any the wiser. Indeed, when she happened to wake in the moonlight, she could hardly resist the temptation. But there was the sad difficulty of getting into it. She had as great a dread of the air as some children have of the water. For the slightest gust of wind would blow her away; and a gust might arise in the stillest moment. And if she gave herself a push towards the water and just failed of reaching it, her situation would be dreadfully awkward, irrespective of the wind; for at best there she would have to remain, suspended in her nightgown, till she was seen and angled for by somebody from the window.

'Oh, if I had my gravity,' thought she, contemplating the water, 'I would flash off this balcony like a long white sea bird, headlong into the darling wetness. Heigh-ho!'

This was the only consideration that made her wish to be like other people.

It must have been about this time that the son of a King who lived a thousand miles from Lagobel set out to look for the daughter of a Queen. He travelled far and wide, but as sure as he found a Princess, he found some fault in her. Of course he could not marry a mere woman, however beautiful; and there was no Princess to be found worthy of him. Whether the Prince was so near perfection that he had a right to demand perfection itself, I cannot pretend to say. All I know is that he was a fine, handsome, brave, generous, well-bred and well-behaved youth, as all Princes are.

In his wanderings he had come across some reports about our Princess; but, as everybody said she was bewitched, he never dreamed that she could bewitch him. For what, indeed, could a Prince do with a Princess that had lost her gravity? Who could tell what she might not lose next? She might lose her visibility, or her tangibility, or, in short, the power of making impressions upon the radical sensorium, so that he should never be able to tell whether she was dead or alive. Of course he made no further inquiries about her.

One day he lost sight of his retinue in a great forest. These forests are very useful in delivering Princes from their courtiers, like a sieve that keeps back the bran. Then the Princes get away to follow their fortunes. In this they have the advantage of the Princesses, who are forced to marry before they have had a bit of fun. I wish our Princesses got lost in a forest sometimes.

After travelling for another hour, his horse, quite worn out with long labour and lack of food, fell and was unable to rise again. So he continued his journey on foot. At length he entered another wood – not a wild forest, but a civilized wood, through which a footpath led him to the side of a lake. Along this path the Prince pursued his way through the gathering darkness. Suddenly he paused and listened. Strange sounds came across the water. It was, in fact, the Princess laughing. Now, there was something odd in her laugh, as I have already hinted; for the hatching of a real hearty laugh requires the incubation of gravity; and perhaps this was how the Prince mistook the laughter for screaming. Looking over the lake, he saw something white in the water, and in an instant he had torn off his tunic, kicked off his sandals and plunged in. He soon reached the white object and found that it was a woman. There was not light enough to show that she was a Princess, but quite enough to show that she was a lady, for it does not want much light to see that.

Now, I cannot tell how it came about – whether she pretended to be drowning, or whether he frightened her, or caught her so as to embarrass her – but certainly he brought her to shore in a fashion ignominious to a swimmer, and more nearly drowned than she had ever expected to be; for the water had got into her throat as often as she had tried to speak.

At the place to which he bore her, the bank was only a foot or two above the water; so he gave her a strong lift out of the water, to lay her on the bank. But, her gravitation ceasing the moment she left the water, away she went up into the air, scolding and screaming.

'You naughty, *naughty*, NAUGHTY, NAUGHTY man!' she cried.

No one had ever succeeded in putting her into a passion before. When the Prince saw her ascend, he thought he must have been bewitched and have mistaken a great swan for a lady.

But the Princess caught hold of the topmost cone upon a lofty fir. This came off; but she caught at another and, in fact, stopped herself by gathering cones, dropping them as the stalks gave way. The Prince, meantime, stood in the water, staring, and forgetting to get out. But, the Princess disappearing, he scrambled on shore and went in the direction of the tree. There he found her climbing down one of the branches towards the stem. But in the darkness of the wood the Prince continued in some bewilderment as to what the phenomenon could be, until, reaching the ground and seeing him standing there, she caught hold of him, and said,

'I'll tell Papa.'

'Oh, no, you won't!' returned the Prince.

'Yes, I will,' she persisted. 'What business had you to pull me down out of the water and throw me to the bottom of the air? I never did you any harm.'

'Pardon me. I did not mean to hurt you.'

'I don't believe you have any brains; and that is a worse loss than your wretched gravity. I pity you.'

The Prince now saw that he had come upon the bewitched Princess and had already offended her. But before he could think what to say next, she burst out angrily, giving a stamp with her foot that would have sent her aloft again but for the hold she had of his arm.

'Put me up directly.'

'Put you up where, you beauty?' asked the Prince.

He had fallen in love with her almost, already; for her anger made her more charming than anyone else had ever beheld her, and, as far as he could see, which certainly was not far, she had not a single fault about her, except, of course, that she had not any gravity. No Prince, however, would judge a Princess by weight. The loveliness of her foot he would hardly estimate by the depth of the impression it could make in mud.

'Put you up where, you beauty?' asked the Prince again.

'In the water, you stupid!' answered the Princess.

'Come then,' said the Prince.

The condition of her dress, increasing her usual difficulty in walking, compelled her to cling to him; and he could hardly persuade himself that he was not in a delightful dream, notwithstanding the torrent of musical abuse with which she overwhelmed him. The Prince being therefore in no hurry, they came upon the lake at quite another part, where the bank was twenty-five feet high at least; and when they had reached the edge, he turned towards the Princess and said,

'How am I to put you in?'

'That is your business,' she answered, quite snappishly. 'You took me out – put me in again.'

'Very well,' said the Prince; and, catching her up in his arms, he sprang with her from the rock. The Princess had just time to give one delighted shriek of laughter before the water closed over them. When they came to the surface, she found that for a moment or two she could not even laugh, for she had gone down with such a rush that it was with difficulty she recovered her breath. The instant they reached the surface –

'How do you like falling in?' said the Prince.

After some effort the Princess panted out,

'Is that what you call *falling in*?'

'Yes,' answered the Prince, 'I should think it a very tolerable specimen.'

'It seemed to me like going up,' rejoined she.

'My feeling was certainly one of elevation too,' the Prince conceded.

The Princess did not appear to understand him, for she retorted his question:

'How do *you* like falling in?' said the Princess.

'Beyond everything,' answered he, 'for I have fallen in with the only perfect creature I ever saw.'

'No more of that: I am tired of it,' said the Princess.

Perhaps she shared her father's aversion to punning.

'Don't you like falling in, then?' said the Prince.

'It is the most delightful fun I ever had in my life,' answered she. 'I never fell before. I wish I could learn. To think I am the only person in my father's kingdom that can't fall!'

Here the poor Princess looked almost sad.

'I shall be most happy to fall in with you any time you like,' said the Prince devotedly.

'Thank you. I don't know. Perhaps it would not be proper. But I don't care. At all events, as we have fallen in, let us have a swim together.'

'With all my heart,' responded the Prince.

And away they went, swimming, and diving, and floating, until at last they heard cries along the shore and saw lights glancing in all directions. It was now quite late, and there was no moon.

'I must go home,' said the Princess. 'I am very sorry for this is delightful.'

'Will you be in the lake tomorrow night?' the Prince ventured to ask.

'To be sure, I will. I don't think so. Perhaps,' was the Princess's somewhat strange answer.

But the Prince was intelligent enough not to press her further, and merely whispered, as he gave her the parting lift up to her balcony, 'Don't tell.' The only answer the Princess returned was a roguish look. She was already a yard above his head.

Night after night they met and swam about in the dark, clear lake, where such was the Prince's gladness that (whether the Princess's way of looking at things infected him or he was actually getting light-hearted) he often fancied that he was swimming in the sky instead of the lake. But when he talked about being in heaven, the Princess laughed at him dreadfully.

When the moon came, she brought them fresh pleasure.

Everything looked strange and new in her light, with an old, withered, yet unfading newness. When the moon was nearly full, one of their great delights was to dive deep in the water and then, turning round, look up through it at the great blot of light close above them, shimmering and trembling and wavering, spreading and contracting, seeming to melt away and again grow solid. Then they would shoot up through the blot, and lo! there was the moon, far off, clear and steady and cold, and very lovely, at the bottom of a deeper and bluer lake than theirs, as the Princess said.

The Prince soon found out that while in the water the Princess was very like other people. And, besides this, she was not so forward in her questions or pert in her replies at sea as on shore. Neither did she laugh so much; and when she did laugh, it was more gently. She seemed altogether more modest and maidenly in the water than out of it. But when the Prince, who had really fallen in love when he fell in the lake, began to talk to her about love, she always turned her head towards him and laughed. After a while she began to look puzzled, as if she were trying to understand what he meant, but could not – revealing a notion that he meant something. But as soon as ever she left the lake, she was so altered that the Prince said to himself, 'If I marry her, I see no help for it: we must turn merman and mermaid, and go out to sea at once.'

The Princess's pleasure in the lake had grown to a passion, and she could scarcely bear to be out of it for an hour. Imagine, then, her consternation when, diving with the Prince one night, a sudden suspicion seized her that the lake was not so deep as it used to be. The Prince could not imagine what had happened. She shot to the surface and, without a word, swam at full speed towards the higher side of the lake. He followed, begging to know if she was ill or what was the matter. She never turned her head or took the smallest notice of his question. Arrived at the shore, she coasted the rocks with minute inspection. But she was not able to come to a conclusion, for the moon was very small and so she could not see well. She turned, therefore, and swam home, without saying a word to explain her conduct to the Prince, of whose presence she seemed no longer conscious. He withdrew, in great perplexity and distress, to the cave in which he lived.

Next day she made many observations, which, alas! strengthened her fears. She saw that the banks were too dry, and that the grass on the shore and the trailing plants on the rocks were withering away. She caused marks to be made along the borders and examined them, day after day, in all directions of the wind, till at last the horrible idea became a certain fact – that the surface of the lake was slowly sinking.

The poor Princess nearly went out of the little mind she had. It was awful to her to see the lake, which she loved more than any living thing, lie dying before her eyes. It sank away, slowly vanishing. The tops of rocks that had never been seen till now began to appear far down in the clear water. Before long they were dry in the sun. It was fearful to think of the mud that would soon lie there baking and festering, full of lovely creatures dying and ugly creatures coming to life, like the unmaking of a world. And how hot the sun would be without the lake! She could not bear to swim in it any more and began to pine away. Her life seemed bound up with it; and ever, as the lake sank, she pined. People said she would not live an hour after the lake was gone.

But she never cried.

Now, the fact was that the old Princess was at the root of the mischief. When she heard that her niece found more pleasure in the water than anyone else had out of it, she went into a rage and cursed herself for her want of foresight.

'But,' said she, 'I will soon set all right. The King and the people shall die of thirst; their brains shall boil and frizzle in their skulls before I will lose my revenge.'

And she laughed a ferocious laugh that made the hairs on the back of her black cat stand erect with terror.

The lake went on sinking. Small slimy spots began to appear, which glittered steadily amidst the changeful shine of the water. These grew to broad patches of mud, which widened and spread, with rocks here and there, and floundering fishes and crawling eels swarming. The people went everywhere catching these and looking for anything that might have dropped from the Royal boats.

At length the lake was all but gone, only a few of the deepest pools remaining unexhausted.

It happened one day that a party of youngsters found themselves on the brink of one of these pools in the very centre of the lake. It was a rocky basin of considerable depth. Looking in, they saw at the bottom something that shone yellow in the sun. A little boy jumped in and dived for it. It was a plate of gold covered with writing. They carried it to the King.

On one side of it stood these words:

> Death alone from death can save.
> Love is death, and so is brave.
> Love can fill the deepest grave.
> Love loves on beneath the wave.

Now this was enigmatical enough to the King and courtiers. But the reverse of the plate explained it a little. Its writing amounted to this:

If the lake should disappear, they must find the hole through which the water ran. But it would be useless to try to stop it by any ordinary means. There was but one effectual mode: the body of a living man could alone stanch the flow. The man must give himself of his own will; and the lake must take his life as it filled. Otherwise the offering would be of no avail. If the nation could not provide one hero, it was time it should perish.

This was a very disheartening revelation to the King – not

that he was unwilling to sacrifice a subject, but that he was hopeless of finding a man willing to sacrifice himself. No time was to be lost, however, for the Princess was lying motionless on her bed and taking no nourishment but lake water, which was now none of the best. Therefore the King caused the contents of the wonderful plate of gold to be published throughout the country.

No one, however, came forward.

The Prince, having gone several days' journey into the forest to consult a hermit whom he had met there on his way to Lagobel, knew nothing of the oracle till his return.

When he had acquainted himself with all the particulars, he sat down and thought,

'She will die if I don't do it, and life would be nothing to me without her; so I shall lose nothing by doing it. And life will be pleasant to her as ever, for she will soon forget me. And there will be so much more beauty and happiness in the world! – To be sure, I shall not see it.' (Here the poor Prince gave a sigh.) 'How lovely the lake will be in the moonlight, with that glorious creature sporting in it like a wild goddess! – It is rather hard to be drowned by inches, though. Let me see – that will be seventy inches of me to drown.' (Here he tried to laugh, but could not.) 'The longer the better, however,' he resumed, 'for can I not bargain that the Princess shall be beside me all the time? So I shall see her once more, kiss her perhaps – who knows? – and die looking in her eyes. It will be no death. At least, I shall not feel it. And to see the lake filling for the beauty again! – All right! I am ready.'

He hurried to the King's apartment; but, feeling, as he went, that anything sentimental would be disagreeable, he resolved to carry off the whole affair with nonchalance. So he knocked at the door of the King's counting-house, where it was all but a capital crime to disturb him.

When the King heard the knock, he started up and opened

the door in a rage. Seeing the stranger, he drew his sword. This, I am sorry to say, was his usual mode of asserting his regality when he thought his dignity was in danger. But the Prince was not in the least alarmed.

'Please Your Majesty,' said he, 'I will put a stopper – plug – what you call it, in your leaky lake.'

The King was in such a rage that before he could speak he had time to cool, and to reflect that it would be great waste to kill the only man who was willing to be useful in the present emergency, seeing that in the end the insolent fellow would be as dead as if he had died by His Majesty's own hand.

'Oh!' said he at last, putting up his sword with difficulty, it was so long. 'I am obliged to you, you young fool! Take a glass of wine?'

'No, thank you,' replied the Prince.

'Very well,' said the King. 'Would you like to run and see your parents before you make your experiment?'

'No, thank you.' said the Prince.

'Then we will go and look for the hole at once,' said His Majesty, and proceeded to call some attendants.

'Stop, please, Your Majesty. I have a condition to make,' interposed the Prince.

'What!' exclaimed the King. 'A condition! And with me! How dare you?'

'As you please,' returned the Prince coolly. 'I wish Your Majesty a good morning.'

'You wretch! I will have you put in a sack and stuck in the hole.'

'Very well, Your Majesty,' replied the Prince, becoming a little more respectful, lest the wrath of the King should deprive him of the pleasure of dying for the Princess. 'But what good will that do Your Majesty? Please to remember that the oracle says the victim must offer himself.'

'Well, you *have* offered yourself,' retorted the King.

'Yes, upon one condition.'

'Condition again!' roared the King, once more drawing his sword. 'Begone! Somebody else will be glad enough to take the honour off your shoulders.'

'Your Majesty knows it will not be easy to get another to take my place.'

'Well, what is your condition?' growled the King, feeling that the Prince was right.

'Only this,' replied the Prince: 'that, as I must on no account die before I am fairly drowned, and the waiting will be rather wearisome, the Princess, your daughter, shall go with me, feed me with her own hands and look at me now and then, to comfort me; for you must confess it *is* rather hard. As soon as the water is up to my eyes, she may go and be happy.'

Here the Prince's voice faltered, and he very nearly grew sentimental, in spite of his resolution.

'Why didn't you tell me before what your condition was? Such a fuss about nothing!' exclaimed the King.

'Do you grant it?' persisted the Prince.

'Of course I do,' replied the King.

'Very well. I am ready.'

'Go and have some dinner, then, while I set my people to find the place.'

The King ordered out his guards and gave directions to the officers to find the hole in the lake at once. So the bed of the lake was marked out in divisions and thoroughly examined, and in an hour or so the hole was discovered. It was in the middle of a stone, near the centre of the lake, in the very pool where the golden plate had been found. It was a three-cornered hole of no great size. There was water all round the stone but very little was flowing through the hole.

The Prince went to dress for the occasion, for he was resolved to die like a Prince.

When the Princess heard that a man had offered to die for

her, she was so transported that she jumped off the bed, feeble as she was, and danced about the room for joy. She did not care who the man was; that was nothing to her. The hole wanted stopping; and if only a man would do, why, take one. In an hour or two more everything was ready. Her maid dressed her in haste, and they carried her to the side of the lake. When she saw it, she shrieked and covered her face with her hands. They bore her across to the stone, where they had already placed a little boat for her. The water was not deep enough to float it, but they hoped it would be before long. They laid her on cushions, placed in the boat wines and fruits and other nice things and stretched a canopy over all.

In a few minutes the Prince appeared. The Princess recognized him at once, but did not think it worth while to acknowledge him.

'Here I am,' said the Prince. 'Put me in.'

But how was he to be put in? The golden plate contained no instructions on this point. The Prince looked at the hole and saw but one way. He put both his legs into it, sitting on the stone, and, stooping forward, covered the corner that remained open with his two hands. In this uncomfortable position he resolved to abide his fate and, turning to the people, said,

'Now you can go.'

The King had already gone home to dinner.

'Now you can go,' repeated the Princess after him, like a parrot.

The people obeyed her and went.

Presently a little wave flowed over the stone and wetted one of the Prince's knees.

'This is very kind of you, Prince,' said the Princess at last, quite coolly, as she lay in the boat with her eyes shut.

'I am sorry I can't return the compliment,' thought the Prince, 'but you are worth dying for, after all.'

Again a wavelet, and another, and another flowed over the stone and wetted both the Prince's knees; but he did not speak or move. Two – three – four hours passed in this way, the Princess apparently asleep and the Prince very patient. But he was much disappointed in his position, for he had none of the consolation he had hoped for.

At last he could bear it no longer. 'Princess!' said he.

But at the moment up started the Princess, crying,

'I'm afloat! I'm afloat!'

And the little boat bumped against the stone.

'Princess!' repeated the Prince, encouraged by seeing her wide awake and looking eagerly at the water.

'Well?' said she, without looking round.

'Your papa promised that you should look at me, and you haven't looked at me once.'

'Did he? Then I suppose I must. But I am so sleepy!'

'Sleep then, darling, and don't mind me,' said the poor Prince.

'Really, you are very good,' replied the Princess. 'I think I will go to sleep again.'

'Just give me a glass of wine and a biscuit first,' said the Prince, very humble.

'With all my heart,' said the Princess, and gaped as she said it.

She got the wine and the biscuit, however, and, leaning over the side of the boat towards him, was compelled to look at him.

'Why, Prince,' she said, 'you don't look well! Are you sure you don't mind it?'

'Not a bit,' answered he, feeling very faint indeed. 'Only I shall die before it is of any use to you, unless I have something to eat.'

'There, then,' said she, holding out the wine to him.

'Ah, you must feed me. I dare not move my hands. The water would run away directly.'

'Good gracious!' said the Princess, and she began at once to feed him with bits of biscuit and sips of wine.

As she fed him, he contrived to kiss the tips of her fingers now and then. She did not seem to mind it, one way or the other. But the Prince felt better.

'Now for your own sake, Princess,' said he, 'I cannot let you go to sleep. You must sit and look at me, else I shall not be able to keep up.'

'Well, I will do anything I can to oblige you,' answered she, with condescension; and, sitting down, she did look at him, and kept looking at him with wonderful steadiness, considering all things.

The sun went down, and the moon rose, and, gush after gush, the waters were rising up the Prince's body. They were up to his waist now.

'Why can't we go and have a swim?' said the Princess. 'There seems to be water enough just about here.'

'I shall never swim more,' said the Prince.

'Oh, I forgot,' said the Princess, and was silent.

So the water grew and grew and rose up and up on the Prince. And the Princess sat and looked at him. She fed him now and then. The night wore on. The waters rose and rose. The moon rose likewise higher and higher and shone full on the face of the dying Prince. The water was up to his neck.

'Will you kiss me, Princess?' said he feebly. The nonchalance was all gone now.

'Yes, I will,' answered the Princess and kissed him with a long, sweet, cold kiss.

'Now,' said he, with a sigh of content, 'I die happy.'

He did not speak again. The Princess gave him some wine for the last time: he was past eating. Then she sat down again and looked at him. The water rose and rose. It touched his chin. It touched his lower lip. It touched between his lips. He shut them hard to keep it out. The Princess began to feel

strange. It touched his upper lip. He breathed through his
nostrils. The Princess looked wild. It covered his nostrils. Her
eyes looked scared and shone strange in the moonlight. His
head fell back; the water closed over it, and the bubbles of his
last breath bubbled up through the water. The Princess gave a
shriek and sprang into the lake.

She laid hold first of one leg and then of the other, and pulled
and tugged, but she could not move either. She stopped to take
breath, and that made her think that he could not get any
breath. She was frantic. She got hold of him and held his head
above the water, which was possible now his hands were no
longer on the hole. But it was of no use, for he was past breath-
ing.

Love and water brought back all her strength. She got under
the water and pulled and pulled with her whole might till at last
she got one leg out. The other easily followed. How she got
him into the boat she never could tell; but when she did, she
fainted away. Coming to herself, she seized the oars, kept
herself steady as best she could and rowed and rowed, though
she had never rowed before. Round rocks and over shallows
and through mud she rowed till she got to the landing stairs of
the palace. By this time her people were on the shore, for they
had heard her shriek. She made them carry the Prince to her
own room, and lay him in her bed, and light a fire, and send for
the doctors.

'But the lake, Your Highness!' said the Chamberlain, who,
roused by the noise, came in his nightcap.

'Go and drown yourself in it!' she said.

This was the last rudeness of which the Princess was ever
guilty; and one must allow that she had good cause to feel pro-
voked with the Lord Chamberlain.

Had it been the King himself, he would have fared no better.
But both he and the Queen were fast asleep. And the Chamberlain went back to his bed. Somehow, the doctors never came.

So the Princess and her old nurse were left with the Prince. But the old nurse was a wise woman and knew what to do.

They tried everything for a long time without success. The Princess was nearly distracted between hope and fear, but she tried on and on, one thing after another, and everything over and over again.

At last, when they had all but given it up, just as the sun rose, the Prince opened his eyes.

The Princess burst into a passion of tears and *fell* on the floor. There she lay for an hour, and her tears never ceased. All the pent-up crying of her life was spent now. And a rain came on, such as had never been seen in that country. The sun shone all the time, and the great drops, which fell straight to the earth, shone likewise, The palace was in the heart of a rainbow. It was a rain of rubies, and sapphires, and emeralds, and topazes. The torrents poured from the mountains like molten gold; and if it had not been for its subterraneous outlet, the lake would have overflowed and inundated the country. It was full from shore to shore.

But the Princess did not heed the lake. She lay on the floor and wept. And this rain within doors was far more wonderful than the rain out of doors. For when it abated a little and she proceeded to rise, she found, to her astonishment, that she could not. At length, after many efforts, she succeeded in getting upon her feet. But she tumbled down again directly. Hearing her fall, the old nurse uttered a yell of delight, and ran to her, screaming,

'My darling child! She's found her gravity!'

'Oh, that's it, is it?' said the Princess, rubbing her shoulder and her knee alternately. 'I consider it very unpleasant. I feel as if I should be crushed to pieces.'

'Hurrah!' cried the Prince from the bed. 'If you've come round, Princess, so have I. How's the lake?'

'Brimful,' answered the nurse.

'Then we're all happy.'

'That we are indeed!' answered the Princess, sobbing.

And there was rejoicing all over the country that rainy day. And the King told stories, and the Queen listened to them. And he divided the money in his box, and she the honey in her pot, to all the children. And there was such jubilation as was never heard of before.

Of course the Prince and Princess were betrothed at once. But the Princess had to learn to walk before they could be married with any propriety. And this was not so easy at her time of life, for she could walk no more than a baby. She was always falling down and hurting herself.

'Is this the gravity you used to make so much of?' said she one day to the Prince as he raised her from the floor. 'For my part, I was a great deal more comfortable without it.'

'No, no, that's not it. This is it,' replied the Prince as he took her up and carried her about like a baby, kissing her all the time. 'This is gravity.'

'That's better,' said she. 'I don't mind that so much.'

And she smiled the sweetest, loveliest smile in the Prince's face. And she gave him one little kiss in return for all this; and he thought them overpaid, for he was beside himself with delight. I fear she complained of her gravity more than once after this, notwithstanding.

It was a long time before she got reconciled to walking. But the pain of learning it was quite counterbalanced by two things, either of which would have been sufficient consolation. The first was that the Prince himself was her teacher; and the second, that she could tumble into the lake as often as she pleased. Still, she preferred to have the Prince jump in with her; and the splash they made before was nothing to the splash they made now.

The lake never sank again, and the only revenge the Princess took upon her aunt was to tread pretty hard on her gouty toe the next time she saw her. But she was sorry for it the very next day, when she heard that the water had undermined her house and that it had fallen in the night, burying her in its ruins, whence no one ever ventured to dig up her body. There she lies to this day.

So the Prince and Princess lived and were happy, and had crowns of gold, and clothes of cloth, and shoes of leather, and children of boys and girls, not one of whom was ever known, on the most critical occasion, to lose the smallest atom of his or her due proportion of gravity.

MANY MOONS

JAMES THURBER

Here is one of the most perfect Princess stories of all time, written by one of America's greatest humorists. Who but James Thurber could have imagined the ingenious and outrageous details of court life, and yet combined them with the kind of common sense that reminds us of Shakespeare's 'thinking makes it so'? This selection, originally published in a book of its own, is fast becoming an American classic.

ONCE upon a time, in a kingdom by the sea, there lived a little Princess named Lenore. She was ten years old, going on eleven. One day Lenore fell ill of a surfeit of raspberry tarts and took to her bed.

The Royal Physician came to see her and took her temperature and felt her pulse and made her stick out her tongue. The Royal Physician was worried. He sent for the King, Lenore's father, and the King came to see her.

'I will get you anything your heart desires,' the King said. 'Is there anything your heart desires?'

'Yes,' said the Princess. 'I want the moon. If I can have the moon, I will be well again.'

Now, the King had a great many wise men who always got for him anything he wanted, so he told his daughter that she could have the moon. Then he went to the throne room and pulled a bell cord, three long pulls and a short pull, and presently the Lord High Chamberlain came into the room.

The Lord High Chamberlain was a large, fat man who wore thick glasses which made his eyes seem twice as big as they really were. This made the Lord High Chamberlain seem twice as wise as he really was.

'I want to get the moon,' said the King. 'The Princess Lenore wants the moon. If she can have the moon, she will get well again.'

'The moon?' exclaimed the Lord High Chamberlain, his eyes widening. This made him look four times as wise as he really was.

'Yes, the moon,' said the King. 'M-o-o-n, moon. Get it tonight, tomorrow at the latest.'

The Lord High Chamberlain wiped his forehead with a handkerchief and then blew his nose loudly. 'I have got a great many things for you in my time, Your Majesty,' he said. 'It just happens that I have with me a list of the things I have got for you in my time.' He pulled a long scroll of parchment out of his pocket. 'Let me see, now.' He glanced at the list, frowning 'I have got ivory, apes, and peacocks, rubies, opals, and emeralds, black orchids, pink elephants, and blue poodles, gold bugs, scarabs, and flies in amber, hummingbirds' tongues, angels' feathers, and unicorns' horns, giants, midgets, and mermaids, frankincense, ambergris, and myrrh, troubadours, minstrels, and dancing women, a pound of butter, two dozen eggs, and a sack of sugar – sorry, my wife wrote that in there.'

'I don't remember any blue poodles,' said the King.

'It says blue poodles right here on the list, and they are checked off with a little check mark,' said the Lord High Chamberlain. 'So there must have been blue poodles. You just forget.'

'Never mind the blue poodles,' said the King. 'What I want now is the moon.'

'I have sent as far as Samarqand and Araby and Zanzibar to get things for you, Your Majesty,' said the Lord High Chamberlain. 'But the moon is out of the question. It is thirty-five thousand miles away and it is bigger than the room the Princess lies in. Furthermore, it is made of molten copper. I cannot get the moon for you. Blue poodles, yes; the moon, no.'

The King flew into a rage and told the Lord High Chamberlain to leave the room and to send the Royal Wizard to the throne room.

The Royal Wizard was a little, thin man with a long face. He wore a high red peaked hat covered with silver stars, and a long blue robe covered with golden owls. His face grew very pale when the King told him that he wanted the moon for his little daughter, and that he expected the Royal Wizard to get it.

'I have worked a great deal of magic for you in my time, Your Majesty,' said the Royal Wizard. 'As a matter of fact, I just happen to have in my pocket a list of the wizardries I have performed for you.' He drew a paper from a deep pocket of his robe. 'It begins: "Dear Royal Wizard: I am returning herewith the so-called philosopher's stone which you claimed" – no, that isn't it.' The Royal Wizard brought a long scroll of parchment from another pocket of his robe. 'Here it is,' he said. 'Now, let's see. I have squeezed blood out of turnips for you, and turnips out of blood. I have produced rabbits out of silk hats, and silk hats out of rabbits. I have conjured up flowers, tambourines, and doves out of nowhere, and nowhere out of flowers, tambourines, and doves. I have brought you divining rods, magic wands, and crystal spheres in which to behold the future. I have compounded philtres, unguents, and potions, to cure heartbreak, surfeit, and ringing in the ears. I have made you my own special mixture of wolfbane, nightshade, and eagles' tears, to ward off witches, demons, and things that go bump in the night. I have given you seven-league boots, the golden touch, and a cloak of invisibility –'

'It didn't work,' said the King. 'The cloak of invisibility didn't work.'

'Yes, it did,' said the Royal Wizard.

'No, it didn't,' said the King. 'I kept bumping into things, the same as ever.'

'The cloak is supposed to make you invisible,' said the

Royal Wizard. 'It is not supposed to keep you from bumping into things.'

'All I know is, I kept bumping into things,' said the King.

The Royal Wizard looked at his list again. 'I got you', he said, 'horns from Elfland, sand from the Sandman, and gold from the rainbow. Also a spool of thread, a paper of needles, and a lump of beeswax – sorry, those are things my wife wrote down for me to get her.'

'What I want you to do now,' said the King, 'is to get me the moon. The Princess Lenore wants the moon, and when she gets it, she will be well again.'

'Nobody can get the moon,' said the Royal Wizard. 'It is a hundred and fifty thousand miles away, and it is made of green cheese, and it is twice as big as this palace.'

The King flew into another rage and sent the Royal Wizard back to his cave. Then he rang a gong and summoned the Royal Mathematician.

The Royal Mathematician was a bald-headed, near-sighted man, with a skull-cap on his head and a pencil behind each ear. He wore a black suit with white numbers on it.

'I don't want to hear a long list of all the things you have figured out for me since 1907,' the King said to him. 'I want you to figure out right now how to get the moon for the Princess Lenore. When she gets the moon, she will be well again.'

'I am glad you mentioned all the things I have figured out for you since 1907,' said the Royal Mathematician. 'It so happens that I have a list of them with me.'

He pulled a long scroll of parchment out of a pocket and looked at it. 'Now, let me see. I have figured out for you the distance between the horns of a dilemma, night and day, and A and Z. I have computed how far is Up, how long it takes to get to Away, and what becomes of Gone. I have discovered the length of the sea serpent, the price of the priceless, and the square of the hippopotamus. I know where you are when you are at Sixes and Sevens, how much Is you have to have to make an Are, and how many birds you can catch with the salt in the ocean – 187,796,132, if it would interest you to know.'

'There aren't that many birds,' said the King.

'I didn't say there were,' said the Royal Mathematician. 'I said if there were.'

'I don't want to hear about seven hundred million imaginary birds,' said the King. 'I want you to get the moon for the Princess Lenore.'

'The moon is three hundred thousand miles away,' said the Royal Mathematician. 'It is round and flat like a coin, only it is made of asbestos, and it is half the size of this kingdom. Furthermore, it is pasted on the sky. Nobody can get the moon.'

The King flew into still another rage and sent the Royal Mathematician away. Then he rang for the Court Jester. The Jester came bounding into the throne room in his motley and his cap and bells, and sat at the foot of the throne.

'What can I do for you, Your Majesty?' asked the Court Jester.

'Nobody can do anything for me,' said the King mournfully. 'The Princess Lenore wants the moon, and she cannot be well till she gets it, but nobody can get it for her. Every time I ask anybody for the moon, it gets larger and farther away. There is nothing you can do for me except play on your lute. Something sad.'

'How big do they say the moon is,' asked the Court Jester, 'and how far away?'

'The Lord High Chamberlain says it is thirty-five thousand miles away, and bigger than the Princess Lenore's room,' said the King. 'The Royal Wizard says it is a hundred and fifty thousand miles away, and twice as big as this palace. The Royal Mathematician says it is three hundred thousand miles away, and half the size of this kingdom.'

The Court Jester strummed on his lute for a little while.

'They are all wise men,' he said, 'and so they must all be right. If they are all right, then the moon must be just as large and as far away as each person thinks it is. The thing to do is find out how big the Princess Lenore thinks it is, and how far away.'

'I never thought of that,' said the King.

'I will go and ask her, Your Majesty,' said the Court Jester. And he crept softly into the little girl's room.

The Princess Lenore was awake, and she was glad to see the Court Jester, but her face was very pale and her voice very weak.

'Have you brought the moon to me?' she asked.

'Not yet,' said the Court Jester, 'but I will get it for you right away. How big do you think it is?'

'It is just a little smaller than my thumbnail,' she said, 'for when I hold my thumbnail up at the moon, it just covers it.'

'And how far away is it?' asked the Court Jester.

'It is not as high as the big tree outside my window,' said the Princess, 'for sometimes it gets caught in the top branches.'

'It will be very easy to get the moon for you,' said the Court Jester. 'I will climb the tree tonight when it gets caught in the top branches and bring it to you.'

Then he thought of something else. 'What is the moon made of, Princess?' he asked.

'Oh,' she said, 'It's made of gold, of course, silly.'

The Court Jester left the Princess Lenore's room and went to see the Royal Goldsmith. He had the Royal Goldsmith make a tiny round golden moon just a little smaller than the thumbnail of the Princess Lenore. Then he had him string it on a golden chain so the Princess could wear it around her neck.

'What is this thing I have made?' asked the Royal Goldsmith when he had finished it.

'You have made the moon,' said the Court Jester. 'That is the moon.'

'But the moon', said the Royal Goldsmith, 'is five hundred

thousand miles away and is made of bronze and is round like a marble.'

'That's what you think,' said the Court Jester as he went away with the moon.

The Court Jester took the moon to the Princess Lenore, and she was overjoyed. The next day she was well again and could get up and go out in the gardens to play.

But the King's worries were not yet over. He knew that the moon would shine in the sky again that night, and he did not want the Princess Lenore to see it. If she did, she would know that the moon she wore on a chain around her neck was not the real moon.

So the King sent for the Lord High Chamberlain and said, 'We must keep the Princess Lenore from seeing the moon when it shines in the sky tonight. Think of something.'

The Lord High Chamberlain tapped his forehead with his fingers thoughtfully and said, 'I know just the thing. We can make some dark glasses for the Princess Lenore. We can make them so dark that she will not be able to see anything at all through them. Then she will not be able to see the moon when it shines in the sky.'

This made the King very angry, and he shook his head from side to side. 'If she wore dark glasses, she would bump into things,' he said, 'and then she would be ill again.' So he sent the Lord High Chamberlain away and called the Royal Wizard.

'We must hide the moon,' said the King, 'so that the Princess Lenore will not see it when it shines in the sky tonight. How are we going to do that?'

The Royal Wizard stood on his hands and then he stood on his head and then he stood on his feet again. 'I know what we can do,' he said. 'We can stretch some black velvet curtains on poles. The curtains will cover all the palace gardens like a circus tent, and the Princess Lenore will not be able to see through them, so she will not see the moon in the sky.'

The King was so angry at this that he waved his arms around. 'Black velvet curtains would keep out the air,' he said. 'The Princess Lenore would not be able to breathe, and she would be ill again.' So he sent the Royal Wizard away and summoned the Royal Mathematician.

'We must do something,' said the King, 'so that the Princess Lenore will not see the moon when it shines in the sky tonight. If you know so much, figure out a way to do that.'

The Royal Mathematician walked around in a circle, and then he walked around in a square, and then he stood still. 'I have it!' he said. 'We can set off fireworks in the gardens every night. We will make a lot of silver fountains and golden cascades, and when they go off, they will fill the sky with so many sparks that it will be as light as day and the Princess Lenore will not be able to see the moon.'

The King flew into such a rage that he began jumping up and down. 'Fireworks would keep the Princess Lenore awake,' he said. 'She would not get any sleep at all and she would be ill again.' So the King sent the Royal Mathematician away.

When he looked up again, it was dark outside and he saw the bright rim of the moon just peeping over the horizon. He jumped up in a great fright and rang for the Court Jester. The Court Jester came bounding into the room and sat down at the foot of the throne.

'What can I do for you, Your Majesty?' he asked.

'Nobody can do anything for me,' said the King, mournfully. 'The moon is coming up again. It will shine into the Princess Lenore's bedroom, and she will know it is still in the sky and that she does not wear it on a golden chain around her neck. Play me something on your lute, something very sad, for when the Princess sees the moon, she will be ill again.'

The Court Jester strummed on his lute. 'What do your wise men say?' he asked.

'They can think of no way to hide the moon that will not make the Princess Lenore ill,' said the King.

The Court Jester played another song, very softly. 'Your wise men know everything,' he said, 'and if they cannot hide the moon, then it cannot be hidden.'

The King put his head in his hands again and sighed. Suddenly he jumped up from his throne and pointed to the windows. 'Look!' he cried. 'The moon is already shining into the Princess Lenore's bedroom. Who can explain how the moon can be shining in the sky when it is hanging on a golden chain around her neck?'

The Court Jester stopped playing on his lute. 'Who could explain how to get the moon when your wise men said it was too large and too far away? It was the Princess Lenore. Therefore the Princess Lenore is wiser than your wise men and knows more about the moon than they do. So I will ask *her.*' And before the King could stop him, the Court Jester slipped quietly out of the throne room and up the wide marble staircase to the Princess Lenore's bedroom.

The Princess was lying in bed, but she was wide awake and she was looking out the window at the moon shining in the sky. Shining in her hand was the moon the Court Jester had got for her. He looked very sad, and there seemed to be tears in his eyes.

'Tell me, Princess Lenore,' he said mournfully, 'how can the moon be shining in the sky when it is hanging on a golden chain around your neck?'

The Princess looked at him and laughed. 'That is easy, silly,' she said. 'When I lose a tooth, a new one grows in its place, doesn't it?'

'Of course,' said the Court Jester. 'And when the unicorn loses his horn in the forest, a new one grows in the middle of his forehead.'

'That is right,' said the Princess. 'And when the Royal

Gardener cuts the flowers in the garden, other flowers come to take their place.'

'I should have thought of that,' said the Court Jester, 'for it is the same way with the daylight.'

'And it is the same way with the moon,' said the Princess Lenore. 'I guess it is the same way with everything.' Her voice became very low and faded away, and the Court Jester saw that she was asleep. Gently he tucked the covers in around the sleeping Princess.

But before he left the room, he went over to the window and winked at the moon, for it seemed to the Court Jester that the moon had winked back at him.

THE PRINCESS AND
RABBI JOSHUAH

FROM THE TALMUD

In a parable from some of the world's oldest religious literature – the great books of Jewish law and history called the *Talmud* – we find an ancient Princess who was perhaps 'beautiful but dumb', and a holy Rabbi who knew how to prove a point amid the false glitter of Royalty.

RABBI JOSHUAH, the son of Cha-nan-yah, was one of those men whose minds are far more beautiful than their bodies. He was so dark that people often took him for a blacksmith, and so plain as almost to frighten children. Yet his great learning, wit, and wisdom had procured him not only the love and respect of the people, but even the favour of the Emperor Trajan. Being often at court, one of the Princesses rallied him on his want of beauty.

'How comes it,' said she, 'that such glorious wisdom is enclosed in so mean a vessel?'

The Rabbi, no ways dismayed, requested her to tell him in what sort of vessels her father kept his wine.

'Why, in earthen vessels, to be sure,' replied the Princess.

'Oh,' exclaimed the Rabbi, 'this is the way that ordinary people do. An Emperor's wine ought to be kept in more precious vessels.'

The Princess, thinking him in earnest, ordered a quantity of wine to be emptied out of the earthen jars into gold and silver vessels; but, to her great surprise, found it in a very short time sour and unfit to drink.

'Very fine advice, indeed, Joshuah, hast thou given me!' said the Princess the next time she saw him. 'Do you know the wine is sour and spoiled?'

'Thou art then convinced,' said the Rabbi, 'that wine keeps best in plain and mean vessels. It is even so with wisdom.'

'But,' continued the Princess, 'I know many persons who are both wise and handsome.'

'True,' replied the sage, 'but they would, most probably, be still wiser, were they less handsome.'

THE LONG-NOSED PRINCESS

PRISCILLA HALLOWELL

Here is a modern story, written in 1960, about an old-fashioned Princess who is so real we can all understand and love her. Miss Hallowell has included almost every classic situation in this account of a Royal Family that acts just like people we all know.

ONCE upon a time in a land far from here, a land called Jingle, there lived a King, a King named Angus. He was a good King, a brave King, and a wise King. He loved his kingdom, he loved his people, and he loved his palace – which was large and beautiful – but best of all he loved his daughter, the Princess Felicity.

He loved the Princess so much that he never noticed what an odd-looking child she was. He never noticed that she had what must be without any doubt the longest nose in the world. It was an unbelievable nose. It stretched on and on; but it had a bit of a tilt at the end that gave her a slightly comic look, rather than an ugly one. King Angus saw only that she was slight and straight, she had two fat golden pigtails, she had the brightest blue eyes that had ever been seen in a human face and a smile that warmed the heart of everyone who saw it.

All the people of Jingle loved the Princess. They smiled and waved whenever they saw her galloping by on her little grey pony, her pigtails flopping as she bounced along. To be sure, she didn't look like everyone else – but what of it? Princesses were supposed to be different. Friendly as a puppy, Felicity was never too busy to stop and talk to anyone she met, and if any of the Jinglites was sick she would visit him and bring him cakes and pies and books to cheer him up. She was the happiest child in the world, and she spread happiness wherever she went.

It wasn't only the *people* of Jingle who were her friends. All the animals in the forest knew and loved her. She spent hours in the woods, watching them and making friends with them. The shyest field mouse ate crumbs from her hand; the fiercest bear sat still beside her, grunting comfortably while she scratched his back. Birds sat on her shoulder, and some even perched on the end of her nose, chirping cheerfully.

In fact, the Princess, nose or no nose, was the favourite of the whole kingdom, and woe betide anyone who harmed her. The years went by and she grew up to be a young lady. But nothing changed. She was the same gay, friendly, unspoiled creature she had always been.

One morning the King and the Princess were at breakfast. The King looked up from the letter he was reading, a slight frown on his face. 'Felicity, my dear,' he asked, 'how old are you?'

'Seventeen last month.'

'Good gradious, so you were! Seventeen?' he repeated. 'Are you sure you're seventeen? It seems only yesterday I was pushing you around the palace in the Royal baby carriage.'

'Well, I really am. Don't you remember you gave me Mother's golden necklace? I wasn't to have it till my seventeenth birthday.'

'Of course, of course, how stupid of me to forget.'

'But why do you want to know, Father?' asked Felicity.

'Because this is a letter from King Hammer — you know, his kingdom is just north of ours. He wants you to marry his son.'

The Princess was surprised. 'But I don't know that I want to get married — that is, just yet — 'specially not to someone I've never seen.'

'Of course you must get married. It's the thing to do for a Princess. Your mother always wanted you to. One of the last things she said to me before she died was that I must find a suitable Prince for your husband. And I must say Hammer makes his boy sound like quite a fellow. Listen to this, child.'

The King pushed his spectacles back on his nose and read aloud from his letter.

'"Prince Fustian is without a doubt the handsomest man in our kingdom. He is as strong as a bull and has every possible accomplishment. He can sing, write verse, dance, and of course his athletic prowess beggars description. He can outride, out-fence, outrun anyone in this country, and I venture to say in your country, too."'

'Hmph!' said the King. 'I wouldn't be too sure of that! But he sounds promising, don't you think? King Hammer goes on to say that Fustian wants to come here and pay you a visit and hopes that you will receive him. How about it?'

'I'd love to see him. He sounds very exciting. But, Father, I don't want to get married and go away and leave you.'

'My dearest Felicity, there is nothing in the world that I shall hate more than having you leave me. But when one is a King or a Princess there are some things that must be done, no matter how unpleasant they seem – things that are one's duty to one's country! It is your duty to marry and mine to find you the best possible husband.'

Felicity hung her head and pushed away her cereal, uneaten.

'Yes, Father, you're right. Of course I'll do whatever you say.'

'Cheer up, old girl. If he's anything like his father's description, you'll fall in love with him immediately, get married, live happily ever after and all that sort of rot, and forget about your poor old father. Though if you do, I'll take you over my knee and spank you, married or not married.'

The Princess smiled. 'Oh, Father, you are ridiculous.'

'Very well, when shall we see this young paragon? He says

here he'd like to come a week from Friday. Is that all right for you?'

'Yes, of course. Any time is fine for me.'

'Very well, then, that's settled. Now I must be off, my dear. I have a lot of work to do.'

The King got up from the table, kissed his daughter on the top of her head and walked out, leaving her sitting thoughtfully at the table. She picked up King Hammer's letter and read it.

'Hmm,' she said aloud, 'King Hammer says nothing about whether his son is kind or wise or good.'

Her shaggy wolfhound, Hubert, who had been lying in front of the fireplace, on hearing his mistress's voice came over to her, wagging his tail expectantly.

'Well, Hubert,' she said, patting him gently, 'shall I marry this Prince Fustian?'

The dog wagged his tail faster.

'Oh, so you like the idea,' she said. 'Well, we shall see what we shall see. There'll be a lot of preparing to do before Friday. Come along, we'd better get started.' She got up from the table and, followed by the great dog, ran from the room.

The week before the Prince's arrival passed quickly. Everyone in the palace was in a state of great excitement. The Royal cooks baked their most delectable pies and cakes; the Royal members of the household cleaned, swept, and polished until the palace shone; the Royal dressmakers sewed day and night on a dress more beautiful than any the Princess had ever had. Everyone was working his head off. The Princess practised on her harp and learned three new songs especially composed by the Royal musicians for the occasion.

Not only the palace was buzzing, but the news of Fustian's arrival had reached all the Jinglites, and they went to work, too. Lawns were mowed, hedges clipped, gardens weeded, houses painted. The Royal bandleader went down to the town to teach everyone King Hammer's national anthem. He also checked to make sure that the people knew their own national song. Men who had quite forgotten the second and third verses of *Hail to Our King* went home and relearned them and practised harmonies they had not sung since they left school.

Never in the memory of Jingle's oldest subject, who was one hundred and seven, had there been such a busy week. Friday, the day of the Prince's arrival, was proclaimed a holiday. The streets were hung with banners, and long before the Prince was expected crowds gathered along the road on which he was to come, waiting to cheer the man who might become the husband of their beloved Princess.

The Princess was up early that Friday morning. She was far too excited to eat breakfast, and so, for that matter, was the King. They had hardly sat down at the table before they were up again.

'Let's inspect the palace just once more, Felicity,' said the King anxiously. 'I would hate to think we had forgotten anything.'

They went from room to room; everything was perfect.

'I may as well go up and get dressed,' said the Princess. 'It takes me ages to get into my new dress.'

'Yes, you may as well. That young man should be here in about an hour.'

'Oh, Father, I'm dreadfully nervous. What if he doesn't like me?'

'Fiddlesticks, my dear – what rubbish! Of course he'll like you. The important thing is that you should like him. Run along, child. I'll be waiting for you in the throne room.'

Felicity went upstairs to her room in the tower. She shut the door and went to the window and looked out. She saw the flags and the crowds and heard the band, and her heart beat faster than usual. She went to the mirror, loosened her long braids and started to brush her already shining golden hair.

There was a scratching at the door. She got up and opened it. Hubert, the big wolfhound, bounded in.

'Oh, Hubert, Hubert!' she said, putting her arms around the shaggy dog's neck. 'I'm frightened. He sounds so grand. I'm sure I'm not worthy of him.'

Hubert licked Felicity's face and wagged his great long tail so eagerly that he knocked everything – brushes, combs, perfume, jewellery – off the Princess's dressing table. They fell to the floor with a crash.

'Hubert, you clumsy old ox! Look what you've done! Honestly, you oaf!'

The Princess sounded angry, but the dog knew, and Felicity knew, that she wasn't. She thumped the dog on his broad back, shoved him out of the way and leaned down to pick up her things, for some reason feeling more like her old cheerful self.

Suddenly the door burst open and Lady Violet, Felicity's chief lady-in-waiting, rushed in. 'He's coming, he's coming!' she cried. 'Hurry up and get dressed, Your Highness!'

As she spoke, Felicity heard a roar from the crowds, and the band struck up King Hammer's anthem.

Her lady-in-waiting helped Felicity into her dress, a dress as blue as her eyes. She wove pearls through the Princess's thick golden hair. After the last hook was fastened and the final tiny button fitted into its buttonhole, Felicity looked at herself in the mirror.

'Well,' she said, 'the dress is beautiful, I must say.' She spun around, watching her reflection. 'Look how my skirt spreads out! It's like a big blue bell. Just *look* at it!' she said, whirling like a top.

'Your Highness, please,' said the lady-in-waiting. 'You must remain neat and tidy. Please calm yourself. The Prince will be here any minute and you must not look as though you've been out in a hurricane. Come here and let me smooth your hair.'

There was a knock on the door. The lady-in-waiting ran to open it. It was one of the Royal footmen. 'His Majesty the King announces the arrival of Prince Fustian and requests the presence of the Princess Felicity in the throne room.'

'Tell the King I shall come immediately,' said the Princess.

Her lady-in-waiting straightened the blue skirt, patted it here and pulled it there. The Princess was so eager to go down that she couldn't stand still another second. 'Oh, Lady Violet, please don't fuss over me. Everything's all right, really it is. I must go now.' She pulled herself away from her lady-in-waiting and hurried out of the room.

'Remember to bow your head when you curtsy, and don't run into the throne room. Dignity, my child, is what – '

But the Princess was out of the room and half-way down the stairs. She and her father had rehearsed her entrance a dozen times. She knew exactly what she was supposed to do. She ran down the stairs, followed by Hubert. When she got to the door of the throne room, she stopped and waited for the huge dog.

'Now, Hubert,' she said in a very Lady-Violet-like tone, 'you must behave, too. Remember, "Dignity is what is expected of a Princess's dog".'

Two palace guards threw open the door for her. Putting one hand lightly on Hubert's head, she stood for a moment in the doorway.

'Her Royal Highness the Princess Felicity!' announced the court herald.

The Princess walked up to the throne next to the one the king was sitting on. All the court attendants bowed and curtsied as she walked by. They smiled happily as they watched their beloved Princess. 'How sweet she looks,' they whispered to one another. 'What a picture they make, our dear Felicity and that great shaggy dog! What a lucky man Prince Fustian is!' As for the Prince, when he heard the Princess announced, he bowed so low that Felicity saw nothing but the back of his coal-black hair.

The King arose as she approached him and held out his hand to her. The Princess curtsied to her father and then turned to the Prince, who was still bent double in what must have been the world's deepest bow.

'Arise, Prince Fustian,' the Princess said, as her father had taught her. 'Arise, and welcome to our kingdom.' She held out her hand to him shyly.

The Prince arose and took her outstretched hand and lifted it to his lips, as his father had taught him. He looked at the Princess and smiled.

The Princess looked at him, at his curly black hair, his flashing blue eyes and his gleaming white teeth. Never in all her seventeen years had she seen anyone so handsome. Her heart melted like a pat of butter left in the sun. She fell in love with him immediately.

'Royal Princess,' he said in a deep ringing voice, 'lovely Felicity, this is a moment I have ... long ... been ... waiting ...' His words came more and more slowly and finally stopped altogether.

Felicity waited, puzzled, for him to continue. She paid no attention to Hubert, who stood beside her, a low growl rumbling in his throat. She had eyes and ears for no one but the shining creature who stood before her.

The Prince looked at Felicity again and the smile vanished from his face. An angry frown took its place. 'What is this?' he said, as his father had certainly *not* taught him. 'Is this some trick? I was told the Princess was a beautiful girl, the most lovely in the Kingdom. Who is this – this monster?'

'Young man,' said the King, 'this is my daughter, the Princess Felicity, whose hand you have been bold enough to seek in marriage.'

'*I* marry *her*?' shouted the Prince. 'Ho-ho-ho – in fact,

ha-ha-ha! I marry a girl with a nose like that! Me, Prince Fustian! Not on your life.' There was a deathly silence in the throne room. No one stirred, but the Prince didn't notice. His words rang out loud and only too clear. 'If I want to marry a freak, I'll go to the circus and pick out a good one. That nose, oh, no! That long, unbelievable nose!'

The King was on his feet. 'Silence!' he roared in a voice that rolled around the room like a crack of thunder. 'Guards! Remove this young whippersnapper from my sight!' Two guards sprang forward eagerly and grabbed the Prince by each arm.

'Fustian, if you are not out of our kingdom in one hour, we will issue an order for your capture and execution. Never, never, on pain of instant death, set foot in our kingdom again!'

'Don't worry, Your Majesty, wild horses couldn't make me. The thought that I, Prince Fustian, who could have the pick of any woman in the world, would choose her!'

'Enough! Throw him out!' shouted the King, his voice shaking with rage. 'And see that he leaves the country.'

The guards picked up the Prince and heaved him out the door.

'Kill him! Hang him! Don't let him get away!' cried the lords and ladies of the court. There was a great deal of angry shouting. It was a good thing for Prince Fustian that the guards had thrown him out so quickly. Hubert would have gone after him, except that the Princess's hand was clutching his collar.

The poor Princess. She stood there completely stunned, her face as white as her pocket handkerchief. No one had ever spoken a cross word to her. At worst, her father had sometimes told her to go upstairs and wash if she came to the table with a dirty face. In all her life she had known nothing but love and kindness. She had never thought about her looks. Now she walked down the steps from the throne over to one of the mirrors on the wall and looked at herself. The noise of the court was hushed. Nobody spoke as the girl studied her face intently. Tears ran down her cheeks, but she paid no attention to them. Suddenly she gave a heart-broken cry, put her hands over her face, and ran from the room.

And that was the end of the party. The gentlemen and ladies of the court, appalled at what they had seen, got their coats and hats and silently left the throne room, too horrified at what had happened to their Princess to say a word. The musicians put their instruments back in their cases and went away without playing another note.

The King was left quite alone in the great throne room. He thought of the proud, hard young man. How dared he hurt his daughter! As he remembered the cruel words the Prince had spoken, the King flew into a most un-Royal rage. The shining silverware and twinkling glasses gleaming on the tables loaded with untouched food, all of which had been prepared with such loving care, seemed to be mocking him. He strode across the room and with one gesture swept everything off the nearest table. China, glass, silver, and food fell to the floor with a crash. He went to the next table and the next – crash, bang, smash – everything was swept to the floor. His rage was a terrible thing to see. When there was nothing left to break, he raised his fist and shook it in the direction of King Hammer's kingdom and muttered awful threats of vengeance. Then, calming himself with difficulty, he left the wrecked throne room and went in search of Felicity.

He climbed wearily up the stairs to the Princess's tower room. As he had expected, the door was locked. 'Felicity, my child,' he said, knocking gently, 'may I come in?'

He heard the key turn in the lock, and the Princess opened the door. The King put his arms around her and tried to comfort her. 'My poor child,' he said, 'if ever I lay my hands on that abominable young man, I'll break every bone in his conceited body.' The King was beginning to work himself into another rage.

'It's all right, Father,' said Felicity quietly. 'Don't get upset. I didn't want to get married, anyway.'

The King looked down at her, puzzled. She wasn't crying, but it would have been better if she had been. She was calm enough, but it was as though something had left her, as though a light had gone out of her face. It worried him.

And it worried him more as the weeks went by. The Princess wasn't sick. All the doctors in the kingdom came and looked her over and could find nothing the matter with her. It never occurred to them that the poor little Princess was suffering from nothing more complicated than a broken heart.

She never went out any longer. Her grey pony grew fat from lack of exercise. The people in the kingdom missed seeing her dashing around the countryside. The birds and beasts in the forest wondered what had happened to their lively friend. Why didn't she come out and see them any more? The entire kingdom was upset, and, as a man, they swore that if Prince Fustian ever ventured into Jingle again, things would go hard for him.

But what worried the King more than anything was that after that terrible day Felicity never smiled again. She was agreeable and dutiful, kept the palace in perfect order and did everything she was told. But she never left the palace grounds, and never, never did anyone see her lips so much as quiver in the beginning of a smile. The gay, ready smile that had been so much a part of her seemed gone for ever. The only request she made was that any mirror that she might pass during her day's duties be removed.

The King did everything in his power to cheer her up, but it was useless. He told her good jokes, he told her bad jokes, he learned parlour tricks from the court jester – but he couldn't make her smile, even when the tricks went wrong. He offered a huge reward, and the Princess's hand in marriage, to anyone who could make her laugh. People came from far and wide to try, but they had no more success than the King. It wasn't that she was sad, exactly; certainly she wasn't cross; she just didn't seem to care about anything. The King was in despair about her.

About six months after his first visit, Prince Fustian decided to seek the hand of another Princess, one with a shorter nose and also a shorter temper – but the Prince didn't know that. The quickest way to this country was to cut across a small corner of Jingle. He remembered the King's warning, but paid no attention to it.

'Pooh!' he said in his most Fustian manner. 'Who's afraid of that old man and his stupid threats? He wouldn't dare do anything to me, and, anyway, I'm only going through a tiny part of his land and no one will ever be the wiser.'

That's what *he* thought. He had no sooner stepped on Jingle territory than a small sparrow saw him.

'Hey,' he piped to his wife, 'isn't that Prince Fustian, the man who insulted our Princess and made her so sad?'

'I do believe you're right,' his wife piped back. 'Let's do something about it.'

'You bet your best tail feather we will! Come on. No time to waste.'

They flew away, and the Prince rode on, little suspecting what was going on.

The sparrows flew through the forest, shrilling and whistling. 'He's here, he's on our land, Fustian the wicked, Fustian the proud. Fellow birds of the air and beasts of the woods, arise! Arise and avenge our Princess!'

In a shorter time than seemed possible every living creature in the forest was on the lookout for the Prince.

'The minute he sets foot in our woods, let him have it!' shrieked the sparrow who, even though he was the smallest, seemed to be in charge of the attack.

The Prince, quite unaware of what was in store for him, rode on haughtily, looking neither to the right nor the left of him. It might have been better for him if he had been more alert. He turned his big black charger into the road that led through the woods, thinking what a fine figure he made and wondering whether the moustache he had just grown became him or if he should shave it off before he inspected the new Princess.

The next moment he felt himself knocked off his horse. He fell to the ground with a great thud. Birds of all sizes were darting at him and clawing at him. A huge bear came rumbling up and started to knock him around with its great paws. Wolves and foxes were shaking him and worrying him. He would have been dead in a minute if he hadn't been wearing his full armour and if all the animals hadn't been so eager to get at him that they got in one another's way and found themselves biting one another.

Fustian tried to fight them off, he was brave enough, but it was hopeless. He fell back unconscious, and it would have been all over with him except that just then a farmer drove by in his cart. Seeing an unknown man in great distress, he chased the birds and beasts away. He bent down and gently lifted the injured man's helmet from his head. He wiped the blood from Fustian's face. It was a mess. His nose was broken, both eyes were blacked and his upper lip was swollen to the size of a sausage.

The farmer was terribly concerned about the young man. He started to undo his breastplate, but froze when he saw the coat of arms painted on it. The big F surrounded by a swan, a wolf, and two hyacinths was as familiar to him as his own name. He had seen it drawn on a hundred trees, posts and walls, all over the countryside. It could only belong to one man – Prince Fustian! And the King's orders were that the man who bore this coat of arms, if seen in the kingdom, should be put to death at once.

The farmer looked at the Prince in disgust. He, too, had missed the Princess. She had often visited him and his family and had brought presents to his children when they were sick. But his was a kind heart, and as he examined the young man further he decided that he was so badly hurt already that he, the farmer, could not obey the King's orders and kill him. So, none too gently, he loaded Fustian into the cart and decided to drive him to the palace.

As the farmer drove through the town, the people he met were curious to know who his battered passenger was. When they found out, they followed the cart, shouting that the Prince should be killed. The farther he drove through the town, the larger the crowd grew and the more loudly they shouted for what was left of the Prince's blood. But the farmer was determined, so he paid no attention to them and drove on to the palace.

He came to the palace gates, hammered on them with his shovel and demanded to see the King. When the guards learned that it was Prince Fustian in the farmer's cart, they opened the gates and let him in, but shut them in the face of the crowd, in spite of their angry protests.

The King, attracted by all the noise outside the gates, had come down into the courtyard to see what was going on. The farmer drove up to him, bowed low, and told his story.

The King looked at the still-unconscious Prince and turned pale with fury. He clenched his fists at his sides to keep himself from doing Fustian further injury. While he listened to the farmer, he made up his mind how to deal with this prince whom he hated more than anyone in the world. As a matter of fact, Fustian was the only thing the King had ever hated in his life.

'Summon the Princess and let the people into the court,' ordered the King. 'We will let Her Highness the Princess Felicity decide what is to be done with this – this carrion.'

The people crowded into the courtyard and gathered around the cart. They were quiet now, waiting for the Princess. In a few minutes she appeared. To the people who hadn't seen her in so long she seemed thin and pale, and her nose that they had thought so gay and special now only made her look sad and pathetic. They became even angrier at Prince Fustian.

Felicity walked up to the King. 'Yes, Father,' she said, 'what do you want?'

'Do you see what is in that cart?' he asked.

The Princess looked. She turned even paler as she recognized the man who lay there.

'Fortune has played into our hands at last,' said the King. 'Now you may have your revenge on the man who insulted you so cruelly. It is for you to decide his fate. What you ask, no matter how dreadful, shall be carried out.'

The Princess looked at the Prince and then at her father. 'I think, Father, we've had enough revenge for a while. Summon the Royal doctor immediately and have Fustian carried up to my room. I will nurse him myself.'

She looked at the Prince's two black eyes, his broken nose, and his swollen mouth. 'Poor Fustian,' she said gently, '*you're* not very much to look at now.' As she said this, she smiled. It was a kind, friendly smile. The King saw it, and all the people saw it.

The King groaned and clapped his hand to his head 'Murdering Dragons!' he cried. 'Do you realize what you've done, girl? You smiled – smiled at that worthless lump of conceit! You've smiled in front of the whole kingdom. You know my proclamation. Now it's all to happen again. I must keep my word.'

'Indeed you must, Father, so you must also call the doctor and have Prince Fustian taken up to my room.'

'Oh, why did I bring her up to be so noble,' moaned the king. 'This is awful.'

But, true to his word, he ordered the guards to carry the Prince to the tower room and went himself to look for the Royal doctor.

The crowd heard all this with amazement. At first they were disappointed that Fustian wasn't to be disposed of in some dreadful manner; then, as they walked to their various homes, discussing what had taken place, they decided that the Princess was right and they loved her more than ever.

The Royal doctor examined the Prince. He poked him here and prodded him there. Then he looked up and said to the King and Felicity, 'He's a pretty sick boy, Your Royal Highnesses. I don't know whether or not we can pull him through. It will mean a lot of work for you, Princess.'

The King thought, Ho-ho, perhaps the wretched boy will not recover and everything will be all right.

Now, mind, the King was not an unkind man – far from it – but this Prince who lay unconscious on the bed before him had, by his thoughtlessness, deliberately changed his bright and lovely daughter into a dull, boring, unhappy girl of no use to anyone.

'Oh, I don't mind hard work, Doctor,' the Princess said. 'It will be fun.' Something in her tone made the King look at Felicity. Her voice had a cheerful ring he hadn't heard in months. He stared harder at her. She was smiling; her cheeks were pink; her eyes were sparkling; she looked like her old self.

The King's jaw dropped. Well, he thought, if that's what she wants, she shall have it, though I shudder to think what will happen when and if she cures him.

The next weeks were busy ones for Felicity. She hardly ever left the Prince's bedside. He was very sick, as the doctor had said, and he hung between life and death for several days. He was out of his head and muttered and shouted quite senselessly.

He didn't know who he was or where he was, and he recognized no one around him.

One morning after two weeks had gone by, Felicity, bringing in Fustian's breakfast as usual, was surprised to find him sitting up in bed.

'What am I doing here?' he asked as she put down the tray. 'What happened? Aren't you the Princess Felicity? There can't be two noses like that in the world.'

The Princess laughed. For some reason, she didn't mind his rudeness any more. 'You should have seen *your* nose a couple of weeks ago,' she said.

The Prince felt his nose quickly.

'Oh, it's all right. It's mended now. Which,' she added crisply, 'is more than I can say for your manners.'

The Prince chose to ignore Felicity's last remark. 'What happened?' he asked again. 'I don't remember anything except that I was on my way to Princess Lucinda's in the south country to see if she'd make me a suitable wife. I was cutting across a bit of your woods when I was knocked from my horse by at least ten armed men.'

'Father told you never to set foot in Jingle again.'

'Oh, that was just nonsense!'

'You wouldn't be here now if you'd paid attention to that nonsense. And they weren't armed men, they were only a few birds and beasts. . . .' And she told him everything that had happened.

'Well,' the Prince said after he'd heard it all, 'I suppose I must thank you, though I can't tell you how many girls there are who would be glad to be in your shoes.'

'How do you mean, in my shoes?' asked Felicity.

'Why, being able to look after me, of course. It isn't every girl who has that chance.'

Felicity looked at him thoughtfully, but said nothing.

The Prince looked at his right arm, which was bandaged

and in a sling. 'Since you have me tied up like a Christmas package, perhaps you would be good enough to feed me my breakfast. Come on, girl, I'm starving.'

From then on Fustian improved rapidly – at least, his health did. His manners got, if anything, worse. He was an impossible patient. He ordered Felicity around as though she were his slave. Whenever the King heard him do it, he would grind his teeth in anger, but since it didn't seem to bother the Princess, the King did nothing about it.

To Felicity, Fustian was a big joke. She was no longer dazzled by his good looks, and she was ashamed of herself for having let her feelings get so hurt and for moping around the way she had for so many months. She could no longer take Fustian seriously. But that didn't worry the Prince; he took himself seriously enough for both of them. She looked after him as she would any other sick creature, and entertained him by reading or singing to him – and, mind, she sang very nicely – or playing ticktacktoe or any other game that amused him.

One day the King came into the tower room, a worried look on his face. The Prince was much better and was sitting up in a chair. The Princess was playing the harp and singing him a ridiculous song she had made up on the spur of the moment. The King looked at her and sighed. She looked so happy that he dreaded saying what he had come to say. Felicity stopped her song and smiled at her father. Hubert wagged his tail lazily, and even the Prince was kind enough to say, 'Good morning, Your Majesty.'

The King cleared his throat and began.

'Young Fustian, it is my duty to bring up what I am afraid can only be an embarrassing matter, but proclamation time has come around and I must speak to my subjects. As you know, in my distress over Felicity's health, I announced that whoever made her smile would win not only a large reward but also the Princess's hand in marriage. Though many tried, you were the only one to succeed. It can be said, and may I say I brought it up at my counsellors' meeting, that since you were unconscious when you made her smile you could not claim the reward, but the vote was against me. A King's word, they declared, is sacred. He must not quibble. In spite of what happened, Fustian must be given the reward and the Princess's hand. She is yours. I await your answer, and then I must make my proclamation.'

Fustian glanced at Felicity, but he could not see her face. She was looking down at her dog, scratching him gently behind the ear.

The King held his breath, fearing the worst.

'Your Highness,' said the Prince, for once remembering his manners, 'I am deeply grateful for your offer, but, as you have just said, a Royal word cannot be broken. I have promised the Princess Lucinda to visit her and, if she pleases me, to become betrothed to her. Fond as I have grown of little Felicity here' – at this point 'little Felicity' gave a very un-Princess-like snort – 'I am afraid I must decline your offer.'

The King was so pleased to hear this that he didn't even notice the Prince's colossal conceit. 'Fine, fine, my boy,' he said, coming over and clapping the Prince on the shoulder. 'Spoken like a true Prince and the son of your father. As soon as you are well enough to travel, I will have you sent to the Princess Lucinda's.' The King mopped his brow. 'My goodness,' he said, 'what a relief! I must go now and make the proclamation.'

So the King made his proclamation and everyone in the kingdom was vastly relieved. A few more weeks went by and the doctor declared Fustian quite cured and ready for travel. The King arranged for an armed guard to escort him out of the country, and the Princess ordered new clothes for him, as the birds and beasts had ruined his old ones.

The morning the Prince was leaving, Felicity was helping him pack. She was sitting on his trunk, trying to close it, but it was too full. The Prince watched her bouncing up and down on the lid and smiled. She was a funny little thing; he couldn't help being fond of her.

'Here, let me give you a hand,' he said, and he sat on the trunk, too, and started to do up the buckles.

Felicity was so surprised that she just sat and stared at him. It was the first time he had ever offered to help her in any way.

'Don't just sit and gape at me,' he said. 'You pull when I push.'

After a few more tries they got the trunk shut, and for some reason they looked at each other and started to laugh.

At this moment the King came in to tell them the guard was waiting and everything was ready for the Prince's departure. He was amazed to see his daughter and the despised Prince sitting on the trunk, roaring with helpless laughter.

Hmm, he thought, it's not only birds and beasts Felicity can tame. It's a good thing that young man is leaving.

'Fustian,' he said, 'your guards are waiting for you in the courtyard. I think you had better leave if you wish to reach the Princess Lucinda's by nightfall.'

'Very well, Your Highness. I am all ready.'

'I'll ride along to the town gates with you,' said Felicity.

The King summoned the Royal porters, and the Prince's baggage was carried down. The King and Felicity and Fustian followed and went out to the courtyard.

The Prince mounted his big black charger and made what was for him an amazingly polite speech of thanks to the King.

A Royal groom brought Felicity's grey pony from the stable and she mounted him and they started off, their horses' hoofs clattering cheerfully on the cobblestones.

As they rode through the town, the people watched them and were none too sorry to see the last of the haughty Prince.

They had passed the last house when Felicity looked up at Fustian and said, 'I'll race you to the gates.'

She kicked her heels into her pony's sides and they bounded off. The Prince wasted no time starting after her. His big black charger was strong and fast, but he was no faster than the grey pony, who whizzed along like lightning. They galloped neck and neck, Hubert bounding along beside them, and reached the gates together. They pulled up their horses, who stamped and snorted, anxious to run farther.

'Good-bye, Fustian,' said the Princess. 'Take care of yourself.'

Fustian looked down at the ridiculous little figure on the prancing grey pony. He was really going to miss her. He wanted to say so, but he was not used to saying nice things, so he only leaned down and shook hands and said gruffly, 'Good-bye, Felicity. Good luck, and thank you for everything.'

'I hope Lucinda turns out to be all you hoped for. Write and let us know.'

Fustian had nothing to say to this. He wheeled his charger and rode off without another word. He turned to look back. Felicity saw him and waved gaily. 'Good-bye, good-bye!' she called. 'Don't forget to ask us to the wedding.'

The Prince turned back and rode on. Blast it! he thought, she doesn't have to be so cheerful. You'd think she was glad I'm leaving. That someone might be glad to be rid of him was such an unpleasant idea that he put it out of his mind immediately. She and her long nose, he thought. Pah, I'm off to woo the Princess Lucinda, the most beautiful girl in the world. I am the handsomest man in the world, so she is bound to fall in love with me. I should bother about what that Felicity thinks! And he went on, followed by the King's guard, who had finally caught up with him.

Fustian reached Princess Lucinda's palace by sundown. He was met with great pomp and splendour and was happy to see that everyone was properly impressed by him. When he was presented to Princess Lucinda, he was even happier, because she was indeed the most beautiful girl in the world. She was indescribable. Everything about her was perfect, from her curling black hair to her trim ankles and exquisite little feet. The Prince wasted no time, but knelt before her and asked her for her hand at once.

The Princess, equally impressed with Fustian's good looks, accepted him promptly. They became betrothed and there was a great deal of excitement throughout the palace.

They planned to be married in a month's time. Meanwhile Fustian would stay at the palace and he and Lucinda would get to know each other.

For about a week Fustian was the happiest man alive. All he needed was to look at Lucinda to realize that he was also the luckiest. Lucinda never said much, but he didn't care – at least she didn't chatter away like a certain long-nosed Princess he knew, and she never, never laughed at him. For his part, he was polite and charming, and even though it was quite a strain on him, he cheerfully obeyed Lucinda's lightest wish.

Then one sunny morning he awoke feeling he had behaved perfectly for too long. Something must give way if he spent another day doing nothing but wait on Lucinda, beautiful though she was. So when he met her he said, 'Fairest Lucinda, seeing that the day is *almost* as beautiful as you, how about getting our horses and going on a picnic?'

'I hate riding,' replied Lucinda. 'It makes ugly muscles in my legs. And I hate picnics. Hard-boiled eggs and sandwiches spoil my complexion.'

This was new to Fustian, but he was determined to be agreeable. 'All right,' he said, 'let's go for a walk instead.'

'Walk!' said Lucinda, horrified. 'I never walk! It might spread my feet.'

'Well, how about some tennis?'

'Tennis! Think, Fustian. My hands! My hands that you say remind you of rose petals. Would you want me to get callouses on them?'

'Oh, no, Lucinda. Of course not. I didn't think. What would you like to do?'

'I think it would be nice if you tried sketching me again. I'm wearing my hair a new way. Haven't you noticed? Perhaps if you drew me in profile you might bring out the delicate line of my nose better.'

At the word 'nose' a picture flickered through the Prince's mind for a moment – a picture of a long, tip-tilted nose, a pair of merry blue eyes and a bright smile that cheered him whenever he saw it. But it was only for a moment.

'Of course, my darling, if it doesn't bore you to pose. It gives me a chance to look at you as much as I want.'

This was the kind of talk Lucinda liked. None of this tennis, riding, and picnics for her. Let him stick to talking about her and her incomparable beauty and everything would be all right.

Fustian went off to get his paints, but he gave a little sigh. This was the seventh time he had tried to paint Lucinda, and he couldn't paint for sour apples, as he had found out to his surprise. But that was the way they spent the day. Lucinda posed happily, turning this way and that way, lifting her head and lowering it, doing anything he asked as long as it had something to do with herself and how beautiful she was.

But from that day on the Prince grew more and more restless. Even though she was the most beautiful girl in the world, he couldn't go on spending every day telling her so. After all, he was pretty handsome himself, a fact that Lucinda had apparently forgotten.

'Play me the harp?' he would ask; but, 'No,' she replied, it would split her fingernails.

'Sing me a song,' he said, thinking of the silly songs Felicity had entertained him with when he was sick. Lucinda knew only one song and she sang that off key.

Prince Fustian found himself thinking more and more about Felicity. He couldn't understand it. Why should that odd-looking little creature come into his mind when he was looking at what must be feminine perfection? He couldn't or wouldn't admit that Lucinda was just as stupid as she was beautiful.

Meanwhile, a new Prince had applied for Felicity's hand. He came from the west and was the son of another friend of King Angus's. He was a nice, sensible young man named Harry, with red hair and freckles. He liked Felicity and she liked him, and they decided to get married. Harry was never cross or rude – he was always cheerful and smiled a great deal, and sometimes he got on Felicity's nerves. But she knew it was her duty to get married, and he was a nice old thing, and she didn't let herself think of dark-haired, rude young men who annoyed her but never bored her.

They sent a messenger with an invitation to Fustian and Lucinda and settled down to prepare for the wedding.

The messenger arrived the day before Fustian and Lucinda were to be married. When Fustian read it, something like a firecracker went off in his head. Felicity marry that fat-faced, red-haired boy! Not while he, Fustian, had his strength.

He didn't wait for someone to fetch his horse, but ran to the stable, saddled it himself, and rode off like a thunderbolt. He rode as he had never ridden before and finally reached Felicity's palace. His black charger was white with lather, and it was snorting and gasping for air. Fustian beat on the palace gates and made such a noise that the King himself came to see who was causing such a commotion.

'What is the meaning of all this abominable noise?' he shouted. Then he looked again and recognized Fustian. 'Good gracious,' he said, opening the gates, 'it's you, Fustian! What in the world are you up to?'

But the Prince was in too much of a hurry to explain. 'Felicity. Where is she?' he said. 'I must see her at once.' And he rode into the courtyard, shouting her name.

Felicity was up in her tower room, sorting wedding presents with Lady Violet. Hearing her name, she ran to the window to see what was going on. She was very surprised to see Fustian.

'Hi,' she said, 'what in the world are you doing? I thought you were miles away, getting married. You look as though you were about to blow up.'

'Never mind me,' answered Fustian. 'What's all this rot I hear about you marrying that redheaded lout Harry?'

'Oh, did you get the invitation? Yes, we're going to be married tomorrow – and he's not a lout, and you'd better take your horse to the stable or he'll founder.'

'Stop yelling out the window and come down and talk to me. I have plenty to say.'

'I can't. Lady Violet and I are counting my wedding presents.'

'Well, stop counting them. You're going to have to send them all back, anyway.'

'Why in the world should I send them back? They've just arrived. Look at this lovely diamond tiara,' said Felicity, holding it out the window. 'Your father sent it.'

'Never mind my father now. Where is that freckle-faced, bowlegged peasant, that stupid ox, Harry?'

'Here I am,' said Prince Harry, who, not being deaf, had heard all the shouting. 'What can I do for you? Well, if it isn't Fearless Fustian, the answer to every maiden's prayer. You look as though you'd been having more trouble with our forest creatures.'

Fustian ignored this insult. 'You think you're going to marry Felicity, do you?'

'Yes, I am. Tomorrow at four. Hope you'll come to the wedding.'

'There's not going to be a wedding.'

'Who says so?'

'I say so.'

'Well, what do you plan to do about it, may I ask?'

'Kill you, if necessary. I challenge you to a duel here and now. I have no gauntlet to throw at you, I left in too much of a hurry, but if I had one it would be at your feet.'

'Well, if you had had one, and had thrown it at my feet, I would have picked it up and thrown it right back at you. I accept your challenge.'

Felicity, hearing all this, nearly fell out the window with excitement. No one had ever fought a duel over her before – and Fustian, of all people.

She turned to Lady Violet. 'Here, you finish putting these away, please, Lady Violet. I must go down and try to stop them.'

The King, who had also heard the challenge, was in a great state. 'Young men,' he said, stepping between them, 'you can't just fight a duel like this. There are certain rules that must be followed. You must have seconds and a referee, and it should be fought at sunrise, not at sunset.'

'We cannot bother about rules, Your Majesty. This must be settled at once. Do you agree that whoever wins may marry your daughter?' asked Fustian.

'I suppose so,' said the King worriedly, 'but it's all most irregular.'

By this time Felicity had come down. She started towards the two young men, but the King stopped her. 'No, my dear, do not interfere. This is something they must settle for themselves.'

Like all palace news, word of the duel spread quickly. In no time at all the whole town knew about it. The people hurried to the palace to see the goings-on. Though they had once hated Fustian, they now thought it romantic and gallant of him to rush in at the eleventh hour and try to win Felicity. They were all for their Princess's being fought over. It was the correct thing to have happen. They poured into the courtyard and crowded around the two young men who had put on armour and were circling each other, sword in one hand and shield in the other.

The King held up his hand for silence. 'Are you ready, Prince Fustian? Are you ready, Prince Harry?' They both nodded. 'When I say, "Go!" you may start fighting.'

There was a moment's silence and then: 'Go!' shouted the King.

The two Princes went at each other fiercely. There was a terrible clashing of steel on steel. First one of them seemed to have the advantage, then the other. They slashed and banged at each other as though one must kill the other. The crowd held its breath, watching. Then it became obvious that Fustian was tiring. He had ridden hard all day, and his strength was leaving him. He could hardly lift his sword.

Felicity saw this and realized that she wanted desperately to have Fustian win. Something must be done. And then she did a terrible thing. The two Princes had separated for a moment. Fustian was standing with his head hanging, his sword dangling practically useless in his exhausted hand. Harry was standing ready for his final charge. Felicity, who was behind him, grabbed her father's sword and, before he realized what she was doing, bashed the hilt of it down on Prince Harry's head. Harry sank to the ground.

Felicity stood there looking at the sword in her hand, appalled at what she had done.

The King was outraged. He started to shout at his daughter, but his voice was drowned out by the cheers of the crowd. They were delighted. It was obvious that the Princess loved Fustian, and it was just like her not to stand by and see him killed. If she loved him, they would, too. He had fought well and bravely. A group of men picked up the exhausted Prince, hoisted him on to their shoulders and marched him around the courtyard. Everyone cheered and waved. Another group lifted Harry, who was sitting up by now, blinking and wondering what in the world had happened. They put him on their shoulders and marched him around as well. He, too, had fought bravely, and they cheered him. The fight had excited them, and they cheered the Princess and the King and even Hubert, who, barking his head off, was dancing around Felicity like a great calf.

The King decided that things had gone far enough. He climbed the palace steps and held up his arms for silence. 'Loyal subjects,' he said when the noise had subsided. 'You have all seen what happened at the end of this duel. I cannot allow anyone, not even my beloved daughter, your Princess, to break the laws of chivalry. I am proud that she had the courage to save the man she seems to love, but I must be true to my word. I promised her to him who won the duel, and there can be no doubt in the minds of any of you who that man is. Prince Harry, you have won Felicity in fair fight. I hereby give you her hand in marriage.'

A murmur went through the crowd. 'He's right,' someone said. 'The King is right.'

'The poor little thing.' Another voice was heard. 'After all that, she's got to marry the red one.'

The Princess walked up the steps and stood beside the King. 'What my father said is true, my friends,' she said sadly. 'I should never have interfered in the fight. I was quite wrong. Prince Harry won, and if', she added nobly, 'he still wants me, I will be glad to marry him.'

But Harry could be as noble as the next man. 'My dear Felicity – ' he said. 'Hey! Put me down,' he shouted to the men who still held him on their shoulders. They did, and he dusted himself off and walked up and joined the King and Felicity.

'My dear Felicity,' he began again, 'far be it from me to separate you from the man you love. I'm too fond of you to do such a thing. I wouldn't think of marrying you, but just remember, I did win the fight.'

This was more than Fustian could bear. His temper really was vile. He separated himself from the crowd and staggered up the steps. 'If Her Royal Highness the Princess Felicity thinks for one minute that just because she saved my life that I will – ' And then, fortunately for everyone concerned, he crashed to the floor, completely exhausted. He had fainted dead away.

The King dismissed the crowd. Felicity rushed over to Fustian and tried to revive him. Harry filled his helmet with water from a nearby fountain and, grinning widely, dumped the water in Fustian's face. Fustian sat up, sputtering. Before he could start talking again, the King ordered the guards to take him into the palace and put him to bed. This they did, in spite of his feeble protests.

'I guess I might as well get my things and be off,' said Harry. 'Good-bye, Your Majesty; I hope we will meet again some time.'

'My boy,' replied the King, putting an arm around Harry's shoulder, 'you have behaved yourself in a truly Princely way – which is more than I can say for my daughter – and I intend to write a letter to your father telling him so. I hope this rather abrupt change of plan has not upset you. I should have liked nothing better than to have you for a son, but it seems that it is not to be. Good-bye, Harry, and good luck.'

The King and Harry shook hands, and then Harry turned to Felicity. 'Good-bye, Felicity. I hope you and Fustian will be very happy. If you love him, there must be some good in him after all.'

'Good-bye, Harry. I'm truly sorry about everything. Please forgive me.'

'Of course I forgive you. But I really must go now.' And, bowing low to both the King and Felicity, he left.

'Harry!' called Felicity before he was out of sight. 'Why don't you stop on your way home and see the Princess Lucinda? They say she's very beautiful.'

'Not a bad idea!' Harry called back. 'I might very well do that. Thanks for the suggestion.' He waved to them, turned, and was gone.

The next morning Fustian, completely recovered, was walking with Felicity in the garden. Suddenly he stopped and, looking down at her, said sternly, 'Felicity.'

'Yes, Fustian?'

'This business of your saving my life – it's becoming quite a habit.'

'Yes, Fustian.'

'I don't like it.'

'No, Fustian.' The Princess had picked a large rose and was pulling it apart, petal by petal.

'It must stop.'

'Yes, Fustian.'

'If we're to be married, it is I who am to look after you. Do you understand?'

'Yes, Fustian. I promise faithfully never to save your life again, no matter what.'

'Good. Now that that's cleared up we can proceed with the plans for the wedding.'

Felicity smiled, but Fustian did not see it. Her head was bent demurely and her silly nose was smelling what was left of the rose. She was learning how to manage her haughty Prince.

'Yes, Fustian,' she said.

So once more the palace and all the court prepared for a Royal wedding. This time they said it must come off. And they were right, it did. But there was one little flurry that had everyone very worried for a few hours.

The day before the wedding the Princess received a letter. It was from Prince Harry, and it said:

Dear Felicity,

I took your advice and stopped and paid my respects to the Princess Lucinda. I am still at her palace. You were right, but you did not say enough. Not only is she the most beautiful creature in the world, but she is the kindest, gentlest, and wisest one, too. It is hard to believe my good fortune, but she has consented to marry me.

Since you in one way or another are the cause of my approaching happiness, I would like to do something for you in return. I have just been informed that in the northern-most tip of my father's kingdom there lives a very reputable witch. She can by a simple spell at her disposal change your nose from its, shall we say, elongated state to one of neatness and beauty equal to that of my beloved Lucinda's. It would be a simple matter for me to arrange to have this done for you, and I would consider it our wedding present to you.

Let me know your wishes on this matter and I will attend to them immediately.

Yours, etc., etc.,
Harry

The Princess was very distressed when she read this. She didn't know what to do. She didn't want any old witch fooling around with her face, but perhaps Fustian would want her changed, and if he did, of course she couldn't marry him. She didn't want to ask her father – she knew he would get angry – and she didn't want to ask Fustian, for fear of what he might say. Finally she decided to ask the Jinglites.

She summoned four heralds and instructed them to ride all over the kingdom, asking everyone to vote on whether or not the Princess Felicity should have her nose shortened. The heralds were to collect the votes and deposit them in a large box in the courtyard of the palace. The Princess herself would count them.

In a surprisingly short time the heralds returned, their saddle-bags bulging with votes – votes written on every kind of thing, from the finest paper to little bits of bark. The heralds fairly bristled with them. There were so many that they had stuffed them into their pockets, the cuffs of their sleeves, their hats, anywhere, even the tops of their boots. The Princess ran to meet them. She watched the four heralds empty the votes into the box and then, her hands trembling a little, she took one out and started to read aloud what her people had to say about her nose.

'Absolutely not!' the first one said. 'Utterly ridiculous! Leave it the way it is.'

'Of course not! We love you as you are,' read another.

'Never heard anything so silly. Why look like everyone else?' said still another.

Felicity stood there reading each and every one. After she had read one she dropped it at her feet. Soon she was standing in a pile of bits and scraps almost as tall as she was. And they all said the same thing. No witch was to touch their dear Princess's nose or change it the slightest bit. They said it in a thousand different ways, from a long and pompous letter written by the mayor of Jingle to a tiny 'no' scratched by a sparrow on a dried leaf. No matter how they expressed themselves, the people had clearly shown that they wanted no change in the Princess.

When she had read the last vote, Felicity gave a sigh of relief and, pushing her way through the huge pile, she ran into the palace to find Fustian.

The noble Prince was in the Royal study, playing a game of draughts with King Angus. Fustian was winning – in fact, as Felicity dashed in he had just jumped three of the King's men. He was annoyed at being interrupted.

'Fustian, read this,' Felicity said, handing him Prince Harry's letter.

'Don't bother me now, my dear – can't you see I'm very busy?'

'Please read it, it's important.'

Fustian started to refuse, but when he saw the eager yet worried look on Felicity's face he changed his mind. 'Your move, Your Majesty,' he said and opened the letter and started to read. Felicity watched him anxiously.

'So Harry's going to marry Lucinda. Very suitable match, I should say.' Then, as he read further, his expression changed, his face darkened. 'Of all the colossal cheek!' he shouted. 'I always said he was an oaf. How dare he suggest such a thing! What insolence! He'd better keep his "reputable" witches away from you if he knows what's good for him! Read this, Your Majesty, and see what a perfectly ghastly son-in-law you might have had if it weren't for me.'

'Young man,' replied the King after he, too, had read the letter, 'I seem to remember some remarks you made, not too long ago, about my daughter's nose.'

The Prince had the grace to blush. 'That was different,' he muttered unhappily. 'I didn't know her then.' He turned to the Princess. 'You're not going to pay any attention to this utterly stupid idea, are you? Please, Felicity,' he pleaded in a humble, un-Fustian-like way, 'don't change. I love you just the way you are.'

Felicity, who had been listening to this with growing delight, exclaimed. 'Why, Fustian, you sound exactly like some of the people's votes!'

'Votes? I don't understand. What votes?'

So Felicity explained what she had done and she showed the King and the Prince a few votes she had saved. They looked at them and then Fustian said, 'Well, I hope that puts an end to that bit of foolishness,' and he crumpled up the pieces of paper and tossed them into the wastebasket.

'I suggest we get on with the wedding plans, my dear children,' said the King, glad of a chance to end the draughts game, 'before something else happens to change them.'

'Nothing will change them this time, I assure you, Your Majesty,' said Fustian firmly.

And nothing did. They were married the following Wednesday.

The people of Jingle still love to talk about the wedding. They tell how the King opened the gates of the palace to everyone; they tell about the feasting and dancing and singing that went on for days and nights; they tell of the wonderful presents the King gave to all his subjects; but what they like best is to describe Felicity and Fustian coming out of the palace chapel. Not only were all the people of Jingle there to cheer the Royal couple, but all Felicity's forest friends had come to wish her happiness. They came in a great parade led by Hubert, the Princess's wolfhound – rabbits, foxes, woodchucks, bears, even a skunk or two, and of course all the birds. The people never tire of telling what a picture it was and how alarmed Fustian's family looked when they saw all the wild animals. But of course they always finish the story by saying that never had there been such a delightful couple to see. Little Felicity, her golden hair flying, her blue eyes shining, and her funny little face alight with happiness, was looking up at Fustian. The Prince had never looked so handsome in his whole life, perhaps because for the first time in that life he didn't give a snap of his fingers how he looked. Like everyone else there, he was thinking only of how much he loved his peculiarly irresistible long-nosed Princess.

Oh, and of course the people add, they lived happily ever afterwards. So, for that matter, did Harry and Lucinda.

NOTES ON THE AUTHORS

HANS CHRISTIAN ANDERSEN
The Princess on the Pea

Hans Andersen (1805–75), Denmark's beloved 'Ugly Duckling', was the son of a poor Odense shoemaker and first heard the traditional folk tales at his grandmother's knee. He was an actor, poet, and novelist before he turned to fairy tales. In 1835, after he had published several accounts of his European travels, his novel *Improvisatoren* drew some praise from the critics. In that same year he published *Eventyr* (Wonder Tales), his first book of fairy stories, and followed it with other books in the same vein until 1872. He had the eccentricity of the true artist, but was welcomed in social circles as a gentle and sensitive celebrity. His fresh perception of the old tales, his power of vivid description, and his sympathy for the misfortunes of his fellow men as well as of his fictional characters have made him the world's most famous author of fairy tales. His works stand today as he wrote them, incapable of being improved or rewritten.

WALTER DE LA MARE
The Dancing Princesses

Walter de la Mare (1873–1956) was born in Kent, of French and Scottish parentage. He never went to university, but was given honorary degrees by Oxford, Cambridge, and St Andrews in his later years. Best known as a poet, he published his first book, *Songs of Childhood*, in 1902 at the insistence of Andrew Lang. He worked for almost twenty years as a statistician and was always known as a friendly and independent writer, tied to no literary school. He collected several unusual anthologies and wrote five novels, the best of which is *Memoirs of a Midget* (1921). *Told Again*, in which 'The Dancing Princesses' appears, was published in 1927 and later re-issued as *Tales Told Again*. His stories show his mastery of the supernatural and the poetic, as well as his great gift for improving the old fairy tales.

MARY DE MORGAN
A Toy Princess

Mary Augusta de Morgan (1850–1907) was the brusque, quick, clever daughter of a mathematical genius. The novelist William de Morgan, author of *Joseph Vance*, was her brother, and he illustrated one of her books. She never married, but engaged in various good works, ending her life in Egypt, where she died while in charge of the Reformatory for Children in Cairo. Her fairy tales – collected in *On a Pincushion* (1877, which includes 'A Toy Princess'), *The Necklace of Princess Fiorimonde* (1880), and *The Wind Fairies* (1900) – all have a magical quality which is essentially timeless. Seldom has a writer of Miss de Morgan's stature been so long overlooked, and it is with pride and pleasure that one of her almost forgotten stories is presented in this volume.

CHARLES DICKENS
The Magic Fishbone

Charles Dickens (1812–70) was born near Portsmouth, and became the most popular writer of his day as well as one of the most prolific. Many of his novels first appeared as magazine serials, and hence we often find each chapter ending on a note of suspense. Today many of his books are read by children as well as adults, among them *Oliver Twist* (1838), *David Copperfield* (1850), *A Tale of Two Cities* (1859), and *Great Expectations* (1860), as well as *A Christmas Carol* (1843), which remains the world's best-loved Christmas story. 'The Magic Fishbone' first appeared in the American Magazine *Our Young Folks* in 1868, and illustrates his unique portrayal of comical eccentrics and his inherent kindliness and good cheer. His writing, always rich in symbolism, also contained vivid pleas for social reform and in later years focused critically on the power of money.

ELEANOR FARJEON

The Princess of China

Eleanor Farjeon (1881–1965), the daughter of a novelist, was born in London and brought up in the Bohemian literary and dramatic world preceding the turn of the century. She never went to school, and the nursery governesses who came to her home were told not to bother her. Exposed to opera and theatre from the age of four, reading avidly in her father's huge library, surrounded by an atmosphere of rich imagination, writing her own stories on a typewriter at the age of seven, Miss Farjeon was uniquely equipped for her literary career. At sixteen she wrote the libretto of an opera, *Floretta*, which was produced by the Royal Academy of Music. Her finest literary success was *Nursery Rhymes of London Town* (1916), verses which she later set to music and which are still sung in many English junior schools. She 'found her feet' (in her own words) with *Martin Pippin in the Apple Orchard* (1922) and went on to publish some eighty volumes, among them *One Foot in Fairyland* (1938); *The Little Bookworm* (1955), which won the Carnegie Medal and the Hans Christian Andersen Prize; *Kings and Queens* (1955); and *The Old Nurse's Stocking Basket* (1949), from which 'The Princess of China' is taken. In 1959 she was awarded the Regina Medal for her life work for children. Since the Second World War she has lived in Hampstead, where she continues to write fantastic fiction, poems, music, and plays. 'Joy,' said one critic, 'is the keynote of her work.'

PRISCILLA HALLOWELL

The Long-nosed Princess

Priscilla Choate Hallowell was born in New York City in 1909, and studied at Chapin and Nightingale-Bamford before a sojourn at Barnard College. She now lives in a large Victorian schoolhouse in Andover, Massachusetts, U.S.A., and is the mother of four children whom she calls 'very satisfactory'. Her husband teaches English and Drama at Phillips Academy. An expert horsewoman, Mrs Hallowell has written a children's book entitled *Dinah and Virginia* (1956) about a talking horse, and a boys' book, *Hector Goes Fishing* (1958).

'The Long-nosed Princess' appeared in book form, illustrated by Rita Fava, in 1959 and was an immediate success. It has been read on television and was a prizewinner at the New York *Herald Tribune* Spring Children's Book Festival. Mrs Hallowell's dramatization of the story has been presented on the stage at the Andover Children's Theatre Workshop and at the Boston Children's Museum. The author's lifelong love of fairy tales has not upset her strikingly realistic approach to the ways of fairyland royalty, and she is the rare perceptive writer who can make a seemingly ordinary situation sparkle with fresh life and wit.

RUDYARD KIPLING
The Potted Princess

Rudyard Kipling (1865–1936) was born in Bombay, India, the son of a teacher of sculpture. Educated in England, he returned to India to edit a newspaper in Lahore and always retained his basic journalistic interest in the news of the day. Poet, novelist, and writer of great short stories, Kipling is perhaps best remembered for his books for children, among which are *The Jungle Books* (1894, 1895), *Captains Courageous* (1897), *Kim* (1901), and *Just-So Stories* (1902). 'The Potted Princess', probably adapted from an Indian legend he heard as a child, first appeared in *St Nicholas Magazine* in January 1893. Romantic in his view of imperialism and in his justification of the 'white man's burden', he opposed rights for women and venerated material progress. In 1907, at the age of forty-two, he became England's first winner of the Nobel Prize for Literature. He is buried in the Poets' Corner in Westminster Abbey, between Dickens and Hardy.

GEORGE MACDONALD
The Light Princess

George MacDonald (1824–1905) is probably the world's most famous writer of Princess stories as such. Born in a primitive town in the Scottish highlands and subjected to a strict religious upbringing, MacDonald was poor for the first part of his life, and sickly for most of it. After studying at Aberdeen University he became a minister, then a tutor, and later a professor of literature. John Ruskin and Lewis Carroll were his friends. He was the father of eleven children and at one time toured England with his entire family, producing and acting in plays. He was always a dreamer and a moralizer, and although moralizing is kept to a minimum in his best works, most of them have a dreamlike and allegorical quality. In 1855 he published his first book of poems, *Within and Without*, which earned him the friendship of Byron's widow, who gave him great encouragement. 'The Light Princess', considered by many to be his finest story, appeared in 1863, to be followed by *At the Back of the North Wind* (1871), *The Princess and the Goblin* (1872), and *The Princess and Curdie* (1883), which are the best of a large body of novels, poems, essays, and sermons.

ARCHIBALD MARSHALL
The Princess

Archibald Marshall (1866–1934) was educated at Trinity College, Cambridge, and studied for holy orders in the Church of England, but finally married and spent three years growing a highly specialized garden. He then became editor of the supplement *Books* for the *Daily Mail* and began his writing career, during which he produced over thirty novels. In 1921 he received an honorary Litt.D. from Yale University in America. He was a regular contributor to *Punch*, and his collected writings from that magazine, *Simple Stories* (1927), in which 'The Princess' appears, and *Simple Stories from Punch* (1930), are among the most delightful of his writings. In 1933 his reminiscences, *Out and About*, were published. William Lyon Phelps, in a biography of Marshall, stressed the realism of his writing. It is the solemn absurdity and almost childlike use of language in *Simple Stories* which give Marshall's book its unique niche in English letters.

W. SOMERSET MAUGHAM

Princess September

W(illiam). Somerset Maugham (b. 1874), born in Paris and orphaned at the age of ten, went to live with a clergyman uncle in Whitstable. He stuttered as a child and was bullied by his schoolmasters and classmates. Refusing to go to Oxford because of his affliction, he spent a year at Heidelberg, studied but never practised medicine, and travelled widely. He has written a large number of novels, among them *Of Human Bondage* (1915), *The Moon and Sixpence* (1919), *Cakes and Ale* (1930), and *The Razor's Edge* (1944). His plays, including *The Letter* (1925), and his short stories were very successful. *The Gentleman in the Parlour* (1930), of which 'Princess September' is a chapter, recounts his travels in the Far East. Highly aware of the relativity of human morals, he has always approached the manners of his era with a quick and accurate wit.

A. A. MILNE

The Magic Hill

A(lan). A(lexander). Milne (1882–1956) was born in London and educated at Trinity College, Cambridge. From 1906 to 1914 he was assistant editor of *Punch*. He wrote several successful adult comedies for the stage, and in 1929 produced *Toad of Toad Hall*, a play based on sections of Grahame's *Wind in the Willows*. He is also the author of a classic adult book, *The Red House Mystery*. But it is for *When We Were Very Young* (1924), *Winnie-the-Pooh* (1926), *Now We Are Six* (1927), and *The House at Pooh Corner* (1928) that he is most fondly remembered. 'The Magic Hill' comes from *A Gallery of Children*, a collection of his stories first published in America in 1925. His gift for completely natural dialogue, the simplicity of his plots and solutions to problems, and his ability to keep his writing always on the child's level without a hint of moralizing are only a few facets of his charm and appeal. To grown-ups his writing shows great humour and even genius, but to children he is simply one of the most natural and delightful writers in the world.

E. NESBIT

Melisande

E(dith). Nesbit (1858–1924) was born in London, the youngest of six children, and fast developed into an active tomboy. She attended a convent school in France for a time, and began her writing career at the age of eighteen, producing mostly hack material for magazines – poetry, love stories, and even socialist propaganda. Later she wrote several novels of which she was very proud, but these are forgotten today. She also wrote a wide variety of material for children, in the literary style of the times, until 1899, when she wrote *The Treasure Seekers* (parts of which, like much of her later work, first appeared in *The Strand Magazine*). Andrew Lang immediately recognized the merit of her latest work and gave her enthusiastic reviews and publicity. From then on her fame was assured. In 1901 she wrote *Nine Unlikely Tales* (from which 'Melisande' is taken) and *The Wouldbegoods*, followed by *Five Children and It* (1902), *The Phoenix and the Carpet* (1904), *The Story of the Amulet* (1906), and a number of other books. Her ability to combine everyday doings with magical events, her uncanny understanding of the minds of children, and her vast imagination have won her a permanent place among the world's finest children's authors.

RUTH SAWYER

The Princess and the Vagabone

Ruth Sawyer (b. 1880) was born in Boston, received her degree in education from Columbia University in the U.S.A., and studied at the Garland Kindergarten Training School in Boston. She later helped to organize kindergartens in Cuba, wrote feature articles for the New York *Sun* and did professional story-telling for the New York Public Lecture Bureau. In 1937 she won the Newbery Medal for her book *Roller Skates*. Her interest in Irish folk tales dates back to her childhood, when she first heard many of the stories from her Irish nurse, Johanna, of County Donegal. Miss Sawyer's own retellings of many Irish stories were published in *Outlook* and *The Atlantic Monthly*. In 1945, after many years of collecting and telling stories, she published *The Way of the Storyteller*, in which 'The Princess and the Vagabone' appears. She is one of the few Americans who have perfected the art of retelling the ageless tale with complete authenticity, as well as in words that are vivid and fresh.

THE TALMUD
The Princess and Rabbi Joshuah

Translated by Hyman Hurwitz and included in his book *Hebrew Tales* (1826), 'The Princess and Rabbi Joshuah' comes directly from the *Talmud*. This great work, encompassing every aspect of life, was compiled between 200 B.C. and A.D. 500 by Jewish scholars. It consists of the Mishna, a digest of the law, and commentaries on the Mishna called the Gemara, from the Hebrew word meaning study. As well as religion and ethics, the *Talmud* contains history, folklore, parables, and many poetical digressions which illustrate the laws, called the Haggada, or story. The ancient story of the Rabbi who taught the Princess a lesson was woven into the *Talmud* to illustrate one of the qualities of wisdom.

JAMES THURBER
Many Moons

James Thurber (1894–1961) was born in Columbus, Ohio, U.S.A., and attended Ohio State University. He worked on the Chicago *Tribune* and the *Tribune*'s Paris edition before joining the staff of the *New Yorker*, the magazine in which most of his work was first published. 'Many Moons' appeared in book form in 1943. Thurber's *The Thirteen Clocks* (1950), unfortunately too long to be included in this volume, is one of the world's great Princess stories. The long list of his highly successful books also includes *The Owl in the Attic and Other Perplexities* (1931), *My Life and Hard Times* (1933), *The Last Flower* (1939), *Fables of Our Time* (1940), *Men, Women and Dogs* (1943), and *The Years with Ross* (1959). Choosing every word with genius and precision, Thurber was a unique master of language, wit, and the human situation. He was unquestionably America's foremost and best-loved humorist, and his cartoons and drawings of dogs are unequalled. Although almost totally blind, Mr Thurber continued to write until his death, and in 1960 appeared as himself in the Broadway production *The Thurber Carnival*. *The Times* called him 'the greatest American satirist since Mark Twain'.

OSCAR WILDE
The Birthday of the Infanta

Oscar (Fingal O'Flahertie Wills) Wilde (1856–1900) was born in Dublin, Ireland. He won honours at Trinity College, Dublin, and at Magdalen College, Oxford, where he studied under John Ruskin and Walter Pater. Among his best-known works are the plays *Salome* (1893), *The Importance of Being Earnest* (1895), and *Lady Windermere's Fan* (1892); his novel *The Picture of Dorian Gray* (1891); his poem *The Ballad of Reading Gaol* (1898); and his essay *De Profundis* (1905). His fairy tales were published in 1888 under the title *The Happy Prince and Other Tales*, which volume includes 'The Birthday of the Infanta'. Convicted of libel in 1895, Wilde spent two years in prison, after which he lived unproductively in France until his death. His work shows his great gifts of imagination and whimsy, but even his fairy tales always contain a sharp ring of reality. His brilliance and wit in both the written and the spoken word were widely acknowledged, even though his eccentricity and morals were criticized.

ACKNOWLEDGEMENTS

SINCERE appreciation is due to the following individuals who have helped with the preparation of this book: Susan Carr, Max Gartenberg, Roger Lancelyn Green, and Sylvia Roman. We also wish to thank the agents and publishers who granted permission to reprint works by the following authors:

WALTER DE LA MARE: 'The Dancing Princesses', reprinted from *Told Again* (or *Tales Told Again*), by Walter de la Mare, by permission of Alfred A. Knopf, Inc. Copyright 1927 by Walter de la Mare. Reprinted in the British edition by permission of the literary trustees of Walter de la Mare and The Society of Authors as their representative.

ELEANOR FARJEON: 'The Princess of China', from *The Old Nurse's Stocking Basket* by Eleanor Farjeon. Copyright 1931, © 1958 by Eleanor Farjeon. Published in the United States by J. B. Lippincott Company. Reprinted in the British edition from *Eleanor Farjeon's Book*, published by Penguin Books, by permission of David Higham Associates, Ltd.

PRISCILLA HALLOWELL: 'The Long-Nosed Princess', copyright © 1959 by Priscilla Hallowell. Published by The Viking Press, Inc.

RUDYARD KIPLING: 'The Potted Princess', by permission of Mrs George Bambridge.

ARCHIBALD MARSHALL: 'The Princess', from *Simple Stories* published in the United States by Harper & Brothers and in England by George G. Harrap & Co. Ltd. Reprinted by permission of Hope Leresche & Steele.

W. SOMERSET MAUGHAM: 'Princess September', from *The Gentleman in the Parlour* by W. Somerset Maugham. Copyright 1930 by Doubleday and Company, Inc. Reprinted by permission of the publisher. Reprinted in the British edition by permission of W. Somerset Maugham and William Heinemann Ltd.

A. A. MILNE: 'The Magic Hill', from *A Gallery of Children*, published in the United States by David McKay Company and in England by Stanley Paul. Reprinted by permission of Curtis Brown Ltd.

RUTH SAWYER: 'The Princess and the Vagabone', from *The Way of the Storyteller*, copyright 1942 by Ruth Sawyer. Reprinted by permission of The Viking Press, Inc.

JAMES THURBER: 'Many Moons', copyright 1943 by James Thurber. Originally published by Hamish Hamilton Ltd. Reprinted by permission of Helen W. Thurber, executrix of the estate of James Thurber.